ALSO BY AMANDA HAMM

WEATHERING EVAN

THE 4ᵀᴴ FLOOR LOUNGE

MEET CUTE: 5 ROMANTIC SHORT STORIES

THE STORIES FROM HARTFORD SERIES
ANDREW'S KEY
JEALOUSY & YAMS
COLLECTING ZEBRAS
THE CHRISTMAS PROJECT
HEARTS ON THE WINDOW (EBOOK NOVELLA)

THE COFFEE AND DONUTS SERIES
SAID AND UNSAID
SOFIE WAITS
A PERFECTLY GOOD MAN
NOT COMPLICATED

THEY SEE A FAMILY
THE STUDY GROUP (EBOOK NOVELLA)

LOVE IN ANDAUK SERIES
EVERYTHING OLD
INTO THE FIRE
BY ITS COVER

What Goes Around

Amanda Hamm

ISBN: 978-1-943598-12-0

What Goes Around is a work of fiction. All names, characters, places, events, etc. are products of the author's imagination or are used fictitiously.

1

It was supposed to be a nice day for a walk. It had been unusually warm for May during the week, but Saturday afternoon was a beautiful, breezy, perfect temperature. Ella felt like getting out of the house. She felt like walking around town looking at anything that would make her think of anything besides the one person she'd been spending way too much time thinking about.

There was plenty to see on Main Street, plenty to think about. A deliciously charred aroma filled the air in front of Burger Brothers. Something that looked like a very fun class was visible through the large window of Joseph's Gym. The beat of whatever music was making kids and grownups alike jump around in there thumped through the wall. Ella passed a man walking a dog and two kids on bikes.

She stopped in front of a small shop called Granny's Shelf. A trinket in the window caught her eye. There were a lot of glass objects on display, but the sun seemed to be reflecting only off one, a small bunny. Ella studied the familiar object. Her Grammy Sweet used to have something exactly like it in her house. She remembered thinking it was pretty and feeling special when her grandmother trusted her to hold it carefully.

Grammy Sweet had passed away when Ella was in high school. Her parents had encouraged her to pick out a memento from around the house before they boxed everything up to sell after the funeral. Ella had thought the idea morbid at the time and refused. Now, looking at the bunny in the window, she wanted it. She regretted not keeping her grandmother's, and this one looked so much like it, she knew it would remind her every time she looked at it.

Movement to her right caused Ella to look that direction. A woman she didn't know was jogging towards her. Ella stepped closer to the window to give her room to pass. She noticed someone behind the woman, someone still a block away, someone she *did* recognize. Ella sucked in a nervous breath. It didn't appear that he'd spotted her.

The desire to examine that bunny grew much, much stronger. Ella wasn't hiding from anyone when she grabbed the handle and yanked the door open. She just wanted a better look at the bunny. She took a single step inside the store before she froze. The absolute stillness of the place shocked her. There was no music, no movement, only shelves and shelves of knickknacks.

Then an old woman with a bun appeared from behind one of those shelves and smiled at Ella. "Can I help you with something?"

"I… uh… There's a bunny," Ella stammered. "I want to look at the bunny."

"Go ahead, dear." She nodded in the direction of the bunny, apparently remembering which window had it on display.

Ella walked around as quickly as she could without breathing too heavily on all her fragile surroundings. She found the item she'd been looking for and picked it up gingerly. It was pretty. Tiny rainbows appeared and disappeared around her as she moved it in the light. And when she set it on her palm, she heard her grandmother's strong alto singing "Amazing Grace," which had been her favorite hymn. Unfortunately, Ella realized she didn't have any money with her. She hadn't intended to make any stops on her walk.

She jumped when the door opened and clutched the glass tighter. Thank goodness she hadn't dropped it. It wasn't only the door that had surprised her. It was the man who opened it. Had he seen her after all, or had this been his destination all along?

"Hi, Sebastian." The old woman greeted him fondly. "How's your mom? Is she recovered?"

"Yeah, she's fine," he said. "It was a pretty mild cold. She just didn't want to infect everyone at the card club."

"Well, we appreciate the concern even though we missed her." She smiled pleasantly. "What brings you in today?"

Sebastian didn't answer immediately. Instead, the two of them turned simultaneously towards Ella. They were both looking at her looking at them. Ella felt her face heat up a few hundred degrees.

"Hi, Ella," Sebastian said.

She managed to squeak out something that she hoped sounded like hello.

Sebastian began to walk closer. "What's that?" he asked with a curious nod to her hand.

She'd forgotten about the glass bunny. Even if she didn't drop it, her sweaty hands were getting fingerprints all over it. "A bunny," she mumbled as she put it on the shelf. She set it down gently, but the clink of glass on glass still seemed very loud.

He cocked his head to look at it while he was still a few paces away. "You're not going to buy it?" His eyes moved to Ella as he asked.

Why did he always do that? How did he do that? Sebastian Jones had the most incredible eyes Ella had ever seen. They were light brown, hazel some would say. It wasn't the color though, and it wasn't the thick dark lashes around them either. It was the way there always seemed to be a question behind them. Ella could swear that his eyes were asking permission to look at her, and it was the most unnervingly attractive thing. Every time. She was so nervous she could barely form a coherent thought, let alone get that thought out of her mouth.

"I, um, can't. Not now," she said. "I was just walking. I saw… but I don't… I didn't bring my purse. I'll, uh…" She tried to look at the old woman instead. "I'll have to come back for it later." Ella ducked her head and began walking. She tried to pretend she wasn't aware of Sebastian's eyes following her. Or the old woman telling him to send her regards to his mom. Ella had taken two breaths of fresh air before she heard Sebastian call out.

"Ella? Can I walk with you?"

She stopped but had trouble forming a response to a yes or no question.

"It's okay if you don't want company," he said. "We just seem to be going the same way and all."

She nodded because that was true. They were going the same way. But why? Why hadn't she gone the other way because Sebastian seemed to take her nod as a yes. As in, yes, it was okay to walk with her. She concentrated on getting one foot in front of the other.

"Were you at the meeting last night?"

Ella nodded again. She was part of a young adult study group at her church. That was how she knew Sebastian. They'd both been attending the Friday meetings for almost a year. She'd noticed his absence the previous night, more than noticed it. She spent half the night watching the door and hoping he would come through it. She spent the other half glad he didn't.

"What was the topic?" he asked.

Great. That was something she couldn't answer with a simple head movement. Ella wasn't sure why words were giving her so much trouble. She'd actually been talking to Sebastian a fair amount lately. She went to the meetings with her best friend Ruth, who usually wanted to chat with her boyfriend for a few minutes afterwards. Sebastian had taken to keeping Ella company while she waited for Ruth. Running into him today was unexpected though, and the surprise was throwing her off. "Hope," she said eventually.

"St. Hope?"

"No." Ella tried to remember a few points from the discussion, which as usual had been all over the place. "Hope as in the virtue, how it's not the same as optimism."

"I'm sorry I missed that," he said. "How is it different?"

"It's, um... it's... Optimism is just positive thinking and hope... hope is trusting God even if things don't turn out well, that he'll still be there or... I mean, and that he'll maybe use the bad things for some good. Something like that."

"Hmm. Here's what I'm hoping...." Sebastian let the sentence hang unfinished.

Ella chanced a sideways glance to see what he was waiting for. Her eyes collided with that hesitant gaze. He was waiting to see if she cared enough to ask what he was hoping. "What?" she said.

Her eyes had already returned to the sidewalk, but she saw the smile out of the corner of one. "I'm on my way to get some ice cream. I'm hoping you might be willing to join me."

"I... uh..."

"Just a friendly gesture," he added quickly.

That let her release the breath she was holding. "I guess so," she said.

"Great."

"Burger Brothers?" She pointed. The red striped awning was right in front of them.

Sebastian was suddenly the one having word trouble. "I...uh... I was thinking Ice Cream Shack."

Ice Cream Shack was several blocks away. "But Burger Brothers has ice cream," she said. "And it's right here."

He slowed his steps and studied the window. "I… think… Ice Cream Shack has more options."

"All right." Ella didn't think it was worth arguing about. His choice was weird though because she got the sense there was something he wasn't saying. And it was just ice cream.

They walked in silence for a block or so. Ella was regretting agreeing to come with him. It was too tense now, and she didn't know what she'd done to make Sebastian clam up. He usually did a lot more of the talking. How were they going to get through a snack with no one saying anything?

"Ella?" Sebastian said. "I'm sorry."

"Me, too."

"You didn't do anything."

"Then why… What's wrong?" Ella asked timidly.

"I'm the one who needs to apologize."

"It's not a big deal," she said. She didn't know why they were arguing about a nice offer of ice cream.

Sebastian shook his head. "I lied to you, and I don't want to lie to you." He took a deep breath. "Ice Cream Shack does have more options so I suppose it was more a lie of omission, but… The truth is I avoid Burger Brothers when Luke is working. He won't serve me, and I don't want to cause a scene. Especially not with you there."

Ella felt her eyes widen. She knew someone who worked at Burger Brothers and said Luke had a short temper. She still had a hard time believing he would go that far. She didn't know what to say. "I'll… I'll get cookies and cream."

She sensed another smile even though she was looking at the ground. Sebastian must have understood that she was saying she'd get a flavor Burger Brothers didn't have to justify their destination. "Me, too," he said. "That's a good choice."

"Oh, no. I… I don't…" Ella remembered why she couldn't buy that bunny and why she wouldn't be able to pay for ice cream either.

"What's wrong?" He stopped just ahead of her and turned around.

"I still don't have any money on me."

He smiled again. He smiled a lot, and she liked that. It felt encouraging, not mocking. "I meant it would be my treat when I offered."

"No, I… can't let you do that."

"It'll only be a couple of dollars. Unless you can eat one of those boat-sized…"

She was shaking her head before he finished so he cut himself off. It wasn't the amount of money. It was the appearance. People would talk if it looked like she was dating Sebastian Jones. In fact, people would talk if she was out in public with him. This was already a bad idea.

He may have understood her concerns because he nodded and took a small step backwards. Then he got an idea. "Hey, I think it's just after four." He pulled a flip phone from his pocket to verify the time. "Yeah, why don't we go to church instead?"

"What!? Church and ice cream are like apples and oranges. Only not." Ella knew it didn't make sense even as she said it.

Sebastian laughed. "Which one is the oranges?"

"That's not… I knew you weren't comparing them. I just… How do you go from wanting ice cream to wanting church?"

"Well, church is free." He shrugged. "And they're both something we could do right now. Then you can sleep in tomorrow.

Didn't you say once that Saturday is your favorite day because you get to sleep in?"

As trivial as it was, it still touched Ella that Sebastian remembered something she'd said. She spent a lot of time feeling invisible. "I'm not dressed for church," she said.

"You look beau- uh, very church appropriate."

The back-pedaling was actually flattering. He'd said enough that she knew his first thought. But he didn't say it because it might push the friendship boundaries. Her face was pushing those boundaries though because she felt another blush, especially when she unintentionally thought he looked pretty great himself.

He was wearing jeans and a light blue button-front shirt with short sleeves. The shirt was kind of wrinkled and had a small tear at the hem so he wasn't exactly dressed up. The color looked great against his skin tone. His mom was more fair so he must take after his dad, whom Ella had never seen.

She was wearing a green sweater that she was sure she'd worn to church in the past even if she hadn't put it on with that destination in mind this time. Her argument was weak.

And Sebastian knew it. "Come on," he said. He took a few slow steps and kept talking when she started moving. "This will be crazy spontaneous, right? I bet you only go to church on Saturday when you're planning ahead for something unusual on Sunday."

Ella pressed her lips against a smile. Both at Sebastian selling church as crazy spontaneity and at how well he guessed her predictable schedule.

He was being goofy on purpose and seemed pleased it was working. "I see you trying not to laugh at me," he said. "I'm right, aren't I?"

She only stopped fighting the smile.

"You know what you can do? Don't mention to your parents

that you went already, then predict the homily on your way tomorrow."

"You think he gives the same homily all weekend?" she asked.

"Probably not word for word or anything. But I bet the main points are the same," Sebastian said. "You could nail those and impress your parents."

"Maybe. But I'm gonna tell them because otherwise they may try to wake me up. You said I should go today so I can sleep in."

"Oh, good point." He smiled at her again. "You wouldn't want to squander this opportunity."

She nodded and tried to keep up some light chat. "What have you been doing at work this week?"

"Well, I'm thinking of renaming the customer complaint folder for this month."

"Really?" Ella had genuine interest. She worked for her dad's insurance company and had swapped some amusing complaint stories with Sebastian in the past. "What are you going to call it?"

"I think I'm gonna call it... Rick."

"Wait. That isn't the same Rick you were talking about last week, is it?"

He let out a playful groan. "He will not let it go. I'm like, dude, no one else has ever had trouble finding that link. You're just blind. But, of course, I can't say that."

Ella nodded. She understood well the forced politeness.

"That's what I'm thinking," Sebastian continued, "while I'm writing, 'Thank you for your feedback.' Again. 'We value all customer opinions and will give yours careful consideration.'"

"When pigs fly," Ella finished.

Sebastian chuckled. "I didn't write that either. We are actually working on a minor redesign, but I don't think Rick will be chairing that committee."

St. Jude's appeared in front of them as they rounded a corner. Ella had relaxed enough to enjoy the conversation as they approached. Church was a better destination. Church wasn't romantic. People did not go on dates there.

Sebastian held the door for her as they entered the familiar building. She'd been a member here since she was a kid, and Ella felt at home. She loved that she was expected to be quiet at church. Even when she was enjoying a conversation, it could be tiring. The break would be welcome. She took a seat in a back pew. Sebastian joined her but with a respectful distance between them.

A peaceful feeling settled over Ella. She couldn't deny that she liked having Sebastian near. Sitting silently in the old building, she could do that without stressing over signs he might be interpreting or ways he might try to get her alone. She could simply be content with the budding friendship.

A stray thought took a flying leap into the back of her head and disrupted the peace. People did go on dates to church. They got married there. Nothing was more romantic! Why did she have to think that while sitting next to Sebastian? He gave her one of those gorgeous hesitant glances just then. It was like he sensed something was wrong and instinctively made it worse.

Ella forced a smile and grabbed a hymnal. She managed to keep her attention focused forward during the Mass and not on who was with her. Mostly. She noticed that he spoke loudly but sang quietly. She didn't let his presence distract her though. As they got up to leave, she nearly walked into Sebastian.

He was closer to the aisle and when she expected him to exit, he turned back to her. He nodded behind her and whispered, "Do you want to go that way? I think Mrs. Donnelly has you in her sights."

Ella shrugged off his concern, and he looked impressed as they moved towards the center aisle. Mrs. Donnelly was in charge of recruiting volunteers for just about everything that went on at St. Jude's. And she was good at it. Everyone said that no one said no to Mrs. Donnelly.

As timid as Ella was though, refusing Mrs. Donnelly was one thing she did very well. All the activities the woman presented involved talking to a lot of people, getting up in front of a lot of people, working with a lot of people. Sure, Ella felt as guilty as anyone for not helping at the church, but those were all things she feared more than guilt.

A woman in her fifties edged through the crowded aisle to Ella's side. "Ella Sweet," she said. "What luck running into you. I intended to stop by last night to talk to some young people but got sidetracked. Now I have a replacement opportunity."

Ella nodded a greeting and waited for the point.

Mrs. Donnelly pushed her glasses down her nose to look over the frames into Ella's eyes. "I have the perfect way for you to be more involved. Bingo!"

"Bingo?" Ella repeated. Was she talking about the actual game or just what she said when she got this perfect idea?

"Yes. Bingo is Sunday nights, and I'm sure you know that draws a mostly older crowd." Mrs. Donnelly tilted her head in a concerned expression, but her eyes remained locked on Ella's. "I hate to think of our seniors getting out all those tables and chairs themselves. We only have one guy who comes early and does all of the setup himself. We could really use one or two able-bodied young people to help." Her eyes flickered to Sebastian for a moment, probably as a backup when Ella said no. Or maybe as the "or two."

"I don't..." Ella started.

"Now our one volunteer is very capable and dependable," Mrs.

Donnelly continued right over her, glancing at Sebastian again. "But it's never a good idea to have all your eggs in one basket. He could get sick or have to go out of town. And this really is a perfect job for you. Bingo starts at seven. All you do is show up at 6:30, set up tables and chairs for about thirty people, then go home. It won't take fifteen minutes."

"Oh." Ella found herself thinking about this. Fifteen minutes where she could be helpful without really interacting with strangers. She still felt afraid to agree. Something made her look to Sebastian for support.

"I bet you could get Ruth to do it with you," he said.

A wave of disappointment hit as she realized she'd been hoping *he* would volunteer with her. It was confusing because hope like that could get her into serious trouble.

"Perfect!" Mrs. Donnelly exclaimed. She pushed the glasses back into place. "You and Ruth go straight to the gym at 6:30 tomorrow. Someone will be there to show you the ropes." She moved down the aisle looking like she was chasing someone, which she probably was.

Ella began walking in a daze. She thought she was good at refusing. How was she now expected to show up somewhere without agreeing to show up? At least Sebastian was right that she could talk Ruth into helping her.

When she reached the bottom of the church steps, she became anxious about not knowing where Sebastian lived. If she didn't know which way he was going, she wouldn't know which way to go. Of course, if he knew where she lived, he'd know if she was taking a longer way to make an escape.

"I'm headed this way," he said, pointing away from her house and simplifying the situation.

She nodded the other way. "That's me. I guess I'll see you Friday then?"

"Full disclosure?"

"What does that mean?" She wouldn't see him on Friday?

"I'm the one guy."

Ella covered her mouth and the giggles that wanted to respond to how guilty he looked over that confusing sentence. "I don't know what that means either," she said.

"I'm the one guy who sets up bingo. I wasn't trying to hide it. Mrs. Donnelly kept looking at me like *she* was about to say it," he said. "So anyway, I'll actually see you tomorrow."

"Oh. Uh, okay then. Bye." Ella waved and turned quickly to hide how much that bothered her. Why hadn't Mrs. Donnelly told her? He was standing right there. The woman could have said Sebastian will be there, not some guy will be there. If she'd had all the facts, Ella would have said no. She would have refused clearly and firmly. And then she'd have kicked herself just as hard as she did for agreeing.

2

He knew the story on Sebastian Jones better than anyone in town. The man was prone to violent outbursts. He lured women into relationships and beat them when they wanted out. He covered his tracks well by dating women from out of town. He'd been arrested several times but managed to stay out of jail when the women were too afraid to pursue the charges or testify.

As Sebastian walked towards his house, a woman walking a dog crossed to the other side of the street before she passed him. She might have been trying to keep the dog out of his way, but he doubted it. People crossed the street without dogs, too.

Sometimes the gossip made Sebastian laugh. None of the stories were funny of course, but he had to laugh. The only other option was anger. Showing even a hint of anger would confirm every rumor in every mind, and he would not give them the satisfaction.

The little yellow house was the same place he'd grown up. He moved out for a few years after college and moved back when his mom had to give up her driver's license. They'd somehow gone almost directly from her taking care of him to him taking care of her.

Teresa Jones was petite at about five foot two and had light gray almost white hair. It was still fairly thick but short and full of curls. She was sitting in an armchair with a blanket over her legs working on a crossword puzzle when he came inside. She looked up. "That must have been a big bowl of ice cream."

"I ran into a friend and changed plans," he said.

"To?"

"Church."

"I approve." She smiled. "I don't suppose this friend has a girl's name."

"Ella," he answered, then changed the subject. "Sorry dinner will be late. Let me go see what I can make quickly."

Sebastian went into the kitchen and stuck his head in the refrigerator. After some perusal, he looked up to see that his mom had followed him. Without the walker. She was being really stubborn about that. She hadn't taken a fall yet, but he could see it was only a matter of time. She held her puzzle book in one hand and grasped the edge of the table with the other as she took a seat.

He decided to skip the nagging at the moment. "How do you feel about grilled cheese?" he asked.

"Do we have ham?"

He pulled open a drawer and called, "Yeah."

"Sounds good," she said.

It sounded good to Sebastian, too. His stomach began to growl as he set up the pan and prepared to grill a couple of sandwiches. They were out of tomato soup so he opened a can of peas. Green was healthy, and he could just eat them fast.

His mom sat at the table working her puzzle while he made dinner. She closed it and set it aside when he put the plates on the table. "Thank you, honey."

He acknowledged her gratitude with a nod, then said a quick prayer before shoveling the peas into his mouth. He wanted to get to the sandwich while it was still hot.

Sebastian's mom apparently had a different goal in mind. Information. "What's Ella's last name?" she asked.

"Sweet."

"Oh, Ron's daughter. The insurance agent?"

"Yes."

"I've seen her," she said with a wink. "She's pretty."

Sebastian kept chewing.

"You've mentioned her a lot lately. You like her?"

"I said she was a friend."

"Hmm." She took a smaller bite and chewed slowly.

Sebastian jumped into the lull. "I saw Mrs. Johnson. She said to tell you she's glad you're over the cold."

She nodded. "You have mentioned Ella a lot."

That was probably true and not a question so he said nothing.

"How long have the two of you been friends?"

"A while." Things had progressed so slowly, he couldn't say how long Ella had considered him a friend, or even if she did for sure.

"And, um," she said, poking at her peas with feigned nonchalance, "how long will you be friends before you ask her out?"

"Mom, you're being nosy," he said.

"No. I'm showing an interest in my child's life."

"Except I'm not a child."

She smiled as though his statement amused her. "Okay. I'm showing an interest in my son's life. As you are welcome to do in mine."

He almost choked at the thought. "There are limits, Mom. I promise to *never* ask about your love life. And if you ever do start dating someone, please don't tell me."

"Oh, I'm way past all that." She gave a little chuckle. "But you're not."

"Still limits."

"All right." She took a bite of her sandwich, chewed in silence, then said, "Women like a man who can cook."

"Mom," he warned.

She shrugged. "Just an observation."

An observation that wasn't nearly as innocent or unrelated as she expected him to think. Then again, she probably didn't expect him to be fooled and only wanted to annoy him into giving something away. He made no comment.

"You know, you haven't made me that dish with the chicken and cornbread topping in some time. Do you know the one I mean?"

"I think so," he said.

"That's one of my favorites. Maybe sometime this week?"

"Yeah, okay. I'll put some things for it on the shopping list."

"Great." She nodded appreciatively. "And when do I get to meet Ella?"

Sebastian rolled his eyes at her.

"What? You said I'm not allowed to ask about your love life."

"Exactly."

"And you said Ella was a *friend*." She smiled at her little trap. "So when do I get to meet her?"

He sighed. "Well, as a matter of fact, you can thank Mrs. Donnelly after you meet her tomorrow because Ella was drafted to help set up bingo."

"Wonderful."

"But you better keep your insinuations to yourself," he said. "If you say anything, you'll embarrass her a lot more than me."

"I'll be good," she said. And fortunately, she appeared sincere.

Sebastian knew he had very little chance with Ella. She was amazing. The more time he spent with her, the more power she had to destroy him. But as long as there was any hope at all he couldn't resist heading down that dangerous road.

One of the things that attracted him was her shifting appearance. She had brown hair a little past her shoulders when it was down. But sometimes it was up. Sometimes it was straight and sometimes it was curly. She had several different pairs of glasses and sometimes didn't wear glasses at all. The changes were never drastic. She always looked like herself, but the subtle changes gave off a vibe of disguise, as though there were parts of herself she kept hidden from the world. It made Sebastian want to know the things others weren't lucky enough to know.

Ella's shyness made her seem just a little afraid of everyone she didn't know well. It was strange and perhaps stupid, but that was what gave him hope. If he could gradually get to know her, maybe she would let him break through the fear the way a woman who wasn't used to fear would not.

But that fear also drew out a protective instinct like nothing else. He wanted to get close to do everything he could to keep her safe. The irony that most people would say he was what she needed protection from wasn't lost on him. If Ella let him close, no one else's opinion would matter. It might be a very long time before he got Ella's opinion on the subject though.

Outside of Friday night meetings at the church, he saw very little of her. Most of that time was spent in a group. It did help, but he only got maybe ten minutes of one-on-one time. Getting to know someone at ten minutes a week was slow going. Today had been a lucky break indeed. Dare he believe it was the Holy Spirit that nudged him to invite her to church? It had seemed a pretty random idea even to himself. And that was where he watched her unwittingly volunteer to give him a few minutes on Sundays now, too.

Of course, she hadn't exactly volunteered so he was nervous she'd figure out a way to back out. It wasn't the only thing making him nervous as he prepared to take his mom to bingo. "Mom, please take the walker."

"I don't need it."

"The parking lot is hard as is the gym floor. You don't want to land on either."

She looked at the walker as though it had just insulted her. "I don't need it. I can lean on you if I get tired."

"It's not your stamina that worries me or the doctor," Sebastian said. "It's your balance."

"My balance is fine."

"Your balance makes you cling to chairs."

"I only need a minute to steady myself when I stand," she said. "I can walk fine."

"I'm taking the walker." He picked it up.

"Okay. But people are going to think you're awfully young to use one."

They walked out to his car with him holding the walker and his mom holding his arm. It felt a bit silly. He didn't mind having her lean on him, but he couldn't be at her side the whole time. She might get up for any number of reasons while he wasn't in the gym.

He tossed the walker in the trunk for the drive, and he got it out before he opened the passenger door. He set it in front of her and held it steady. She looked at it, then used the door to pull herself from the seat. When she was standing, she grabbed the walker only long enough to move it out of the way. She walked towards the building and left the walker and Sebastian, and the car door open.

He closed his eyes for a moment. Then he closed the car door and picked up the walker to catch up to his mom. He resumed the position of having the walker on one arm and her on the other.

A couple of car doors slammed behind them a minute before two young women jogged up to join them. "Hi, Sebastian," the redhead said. The other one was Ella. She only nodded a greeting.

Sebastian's mom stopped moving her legs and forced him to stop. Her eyes switched rapidly between him and the newcomers, clearly begging for introductions.

"Hello," Sebastian said. "This is my mom, Teresa Jones."

"Ruth Ziebert." Ruth held out her hand.

Sebastian's mom let go of him to shake the hand, then held hers out to Ella.

"Ella Sweet."

His mom gave no hint that the name had any significance, which was lucky for her. Because if she had, he was going to make her wax beans – her least favorite – for a month.

"You ladies are helping us get ready today?" she asked.

Ruth nodded. "Yes, ma'am."

"Wonderful." She took Sebastian's arm again to nudge the party forward.

The gym was large and empty as they walked inside. "Let me grab a chair for my mom," Sebastian said, "then I'll tell you where we're supposed to put everything."

All three of the women nodded. Sebastian set the walker right in front of his mom with a pointed look that she ignored. Hopefully, if she wobbled, instinct would make her reach for it even if pride didn't.

The space always seemed large, but it seemed larger as he left Ella on the opposite side of it. There was a storage closet at the far end. He opened it and rolled out a rack of folded chairs. When he turned around with a single chair in hand, his mom was already explaining where the tables would go. She was walking around to do it with the walker sitting forlornly where he'd left it. He might have gotten annoyed if the sight had surprised him in the slightest.

Sebastian took a moment to appreciate a more pleasant sight. Ella was following a few steps behind Ruth and his mom. There was a thick braid behind each ear, and she wore the blue glasses with the thin frames. He liked those. As he got closer, he could see her eyes behind them darting around the room. Some of those glances were definitely coming his way. It was encouraging whether she meant it that way or not.

Then out of the corner of his eye, Sebastian saw his mom take an awkward step. Her body pitched forward and her arms flailed. In the very long second that followed, Sebastian knew only that he was too far away to get there in time.

Thank God, Ruth was close enough. She grabbed the older woman's forearm and held on until she got her feet back under her. Sebastian ran the last few steps, unfolded the chair right next to his mom and gently lowered her into it.

She looked up at Ruth. "Thank you, dear," she said. "I nearly got better acquainted with the floor there."

Sebastian forced a smile at the terrible joke instead of yelling at her to use the walker. Concerned yelling might have been mistaken for anger.

"Are you sure you're all right?" Ruth asked.

"I'm fine now. Just took a bad step."

"Promise you'll stay right there while we get the tables out, Mom?"

"I'll show the girls where to put them." His mom moved to push herself from the chair.

"You're content to sit when I do this myself," he said as he placed himself in front of her to block her attempt to stand. "This time I have help."

"I can help, too," she said.

"No." He didn't move.

"The tables are back there?" Ruth pointed at the closet. Sebastian nodded at her.

"We'll get the first one." She motioned Ella to follow her, though she'd already started moving that direction.

Sebastian knew they were trying not to get in the middle of a family thing. He turned to his mom and whispered, "You're making them uncomfortable. Please don't fight with me in front of them."

"This isn't fighting," she whispered back. "And don't treat me like a two-year-old in front of them either."

"I'm not treating you like a child. I'm treating you like a woman who might fall and hurt herself. Our home is mostly carpeted and has lots of stuff to grab." He waved an arm at the expanse behind him. "There's not much here to keep you from getting better acquainted with the floor, as you put it. Except the walker. Would you like me to get it?"

Her eyes moved to the object in question and back to his face. "No, thank you. I'll sit and direct from here."

"Thank you."

Ruth and Ella returned, each carrying an end of the same rectangular table.

"Mom will tell you where to set that up while I get the next one."

Once they got started, the room was ready in a few minutes.

Sebastian was glad to see his mom decided to be a good sport. She called out weirdly precise directions to all of them about tables being moved seven point three inches to the left or rotated forty-seven degrees clockwise. Ella and Ruth were entertained by it since no one expected them to actually be that precise.

Sebastian returned the chair rack to the closet as the last step. As he walked across the gym, Ruth was talking to his mom and no one was talking to Ella. She was maybe ten feet away unnecessarily straightening a few chairs. He approached between the two columns of tables and turned towards Ella rather than go around and risk chasing her closer to the others.

"Thanks again," he said as he got within talking distance. "It really did go faster with help. Maybe we'll set a new record next week." He was taking a page from Mrs. Donnelly's book by assuming she was coming back rather than asking.

"I think that was fast enough. Why do guys turn everything into a competition?" She was teasing, not complaining, and not correcting his assumption.

"Nothing wrong with a little efficiency."

She smiled. She was looking at the back of the chair more than him, but she wasn't trying to rejoin Ruth. "Are you staying to play?"

"What? Bingo? I can hardly think of a more boring way to spend two hours." It was the truth, but he regretted it as soon as he said it. What if Ella had been considering staying herself? It would be far less boring with her there. "Were you thinking of staying?" he asked sheepishly.

She shook her head. "I just asked, um… I guess you have to come back for your mom then?"

"Oh. Right. If I had to be here anyway… But I'll go home and stare at the wall. Much more exciting."

Her mouth fought against a smile. "I'm kind of surprised your mom plays since… um… I mean, some people… never mind." She was turning red.

"You mean because it's a form of gambling, which some people find addictive?" He tried to ask gently because he didn't want to embarrass her for bringing it up. But his mom never tried to hide her past, and Sebastian wanted to be as open and honest with Ella as possible, partly to encourage the same from her.

She glanced up for a second and mumbled, "Sort of."

"My mom was a little wary when someone first invited her, but gambling was never a weakness for her, only alcohol. She still keeps an eye out for warning signs that it might be a problem, mostly by missing a week now and then to see if she feels any anxiety about it. The pots are small and she donates anything she wins right back to the church. So far, she's sure it's just a game she plays to spend time with friends."

Ella had started making eye contact during the explanation. She looked interested and relieved that it was something he didn't mind telling her. "But she hasn't talked you into it?" she asked, finally smiling for real.

"Not yet," he said. "Do you want to try? Tell me how it's fun to sit and listen to numbers."

Her smile stretched into a small laugh.

"What are you doing tonight?"

The laugh stopped abruptly. "I, um… don't know."

Wrong choice of words. He'd sounded as though he was about to suggest something together. He'd love to, but he'd just talked her into church the day before as a friendly gesture. Two days in a row wouldn't fool anyone. And he really hadn't meant it that way. "That was a mistake," he said.

Her eyes widened uncertainly.

"I mean, when I… I didn't mean to pry into your plans. I only wanted to ask what are some things you think are more fun than bingo?"

"Oh. Okay." She looked around the room for answers. "I do like a lot of board games."

"Yeah?" He wanted her to relax again. She said that like she was afraid it was a wrong answer. "What about staring at the wall? More fun than bingo?"

She hesitated, then said, "Depends which wall."

Sebastian laughed hard enough to get his mom's attention. She demanded to know what was so amusing.

"Ella and I are just discussing things that are more fun than bingo."

His mom simply gave a disapproving look. She knew his opinion and could guess what sort of joke he'd made of it. Two women around his mom's age entered the gym then, and Ruth suggested to Ella that they should go.

Ella said, "Bye, Sebastian," and headed for the exit with Ruth. They passed another bingo player coming in.

It was time for Sebastian to get out, too. He helped his mom move her chair to a place at a table, mostly by hovering while she did it. Then he asked her where he should leave the walker.

"Why don't you just take it with you now so you don't have to carry it around?" she asked.

"I know it's a hassle at home, but can't you just use it here? Look! She has one, too." He pointed to another arriving player. "All the cool kids have them here."

Her lips twitched against a smile. "Leave it at the end of the table," she said. "I will consider it for emergencies only."

He wasn't going to get better than that so he left the walker where she suggested and hightailed it out of there before the place got any fuller. On the way home, he realized something. When Ella left, she'd called him by name. He didn't think she'd ever done that before. Was that progress?

3

Monday morning, Ella couldn't wait for her dad to leave. She loved her dad. She got along well with him and was happy to have him as her boss. But she needed to have a private conversation with Ruth and couldn't do that until he left for the 10 AM appointment she knew was on his calendar.

Ella had decided she needed to tell someone. She was going to explode keeping the problem to herself. She wanted to tell Ruth after they set up the room for bingo, but there hadn't been time. She'd already begged Ruth to interrupt her evening with Gabriel to do the setup. It would have been asking too much to delve into a serious issue on top of the other favor.

Ruth and Ella had desks next to each other in the front of the insurance office on Main Street. Mr. Sweet, Ella's dad, had a private office in the back. Most of the time, the door between the spaces was open so it wasn't private enough.

Ella's dad was small for a man, a little short and very thin. He had a ring of hair around a bald crown. He stood in the doorway between offices now leaning against the frame. He held an open file folder and was going over a list to see how their week looked. It actually looked kind of slow, which meant Ella wouldn't feel too guilty about having a little nonwork chat while he was out.

He went into his office to exchange the folder for a briefcase. "I'll probably grab lunch on my way back," he said. "Do either of you want me to pick up something for you?"

Ruth shook her head. "Thank you, but I packed."

"Me, too." Ella hoped he didn't notice her foot tapping.

"All right." He moved to the front door. "Call me if you need anything."

As soon as the door closed behind him, Ella completely clammed up. She was dying to get some advice but not nearly as eager to share why she needed advice.

"What did you think of Joseph and Emily's announcement?" Ruth asked.

"Um…" Catching up to the sudden question confused Ella out of her nerve battle. "What are you talking about?"

"The reception at Burger Brothers?"

"Oh, right. I thought your mom was funny."

Ruth laughed. "Yeah. She was so worried that Emily was upset about it, but it was clearly her idea."

"I know," Ella said. "She was proud of having talked Chip into closing for the night for a private party."

"My brother has always been super cheap." Ruth shook her head but with obvious fondness. "He found a pretty good match, and my mom is still worried it'll drive her away."

"Any news after your evening with Gabriel?" Ella asked.

"No. He's never going to ask me."

Ella offered her best sympathetic smile, under the circumstances. The circumstances being Ruth was dating someone she was madly in love with who had said months ago that he was going to propose soon. Apparently, the two of them had very different ideas of soon. Ella considered her own problem much bigger. "He will," she said, because she did want Ruth to be happy.

Ruth sighed. Then turned her attention to Ella. She must have seen some agitation. "Is something going on with you?"

"Yes. I have a big problem. You gotta help me."

Ruth dropped her pen and turned her chair towards Ella. "What's going on?" she asked seriously.

Ella sucked in a breath and prepared to let it out. "I like him," she said.

"You like him?" Ruth's eyes got big and round. "Sebastian?"

"Oh, no!" She'd guessed way too quickly. "I like him, and it's obvious." Ella was afraid she was going to hyperventilate. It was worse than she thought.

Ruth worked to calm her down. "No, it isn't obvious. I only guessed Sebastian because I know you saw him yesterday."

"Really?"

"Yes, really. But you like him as in..."

"As in I have a serious crush, and I can't because he's... he's Sebastian Jones. The name is synonymous with abusive boyfriend. I am out of my mind. How do I cure myself of this like yesterday?"

"Wow." Ruth just sat there blinking for a minute. "You know, I kind of thought he might have a thing for you."

"That does not help," Ella said. "I'm trying to be friends with him, only friends. I don't want to avoid him because... because other people do. I sat a few rows behind him at church recently and yeah, I did it on purpose. I already admitted I like him. I followed him inside and deliberately led my parents to a seat where I could see him."

Ruth was trying not to laugh at this little speech. Her amusement wasn't offensive. It was making it harder for Ella to keep a straight face.

"So anyway... There was a family on the other side of the pew when he sat down. They started whispering, and after a few minutes they got up and moved. They actually got up and changed seats, and I could tell it was to avoid sitting near Sebastian. In church. And he told me that he can't go into Burger Brothers when Luke is working or he'll get thrown out."

"Luke would really do that?"

"Apparently. Some people treat Sebastian like dirt, and I don't want to do that. I just want to figure out how to not have a crush on him. So when I say I like him, you're not supposed to say 'I think he likes you, too.' That does not help."

"I know," Ruth said. "I never said anything because I thought... well, I thought you might be afraid of him."

"I am. I was. I..." Ella shrugged. Ruth knew about her social anxiety. "I'm afraid of everyone. At first. But ever since I've been seeing Sebastian on Fridays, he always seems so nice. He says things. He talks about God and faith with genuine insight. He talks about taking care of his mom. Jessica lets him hold Grace, and he's so gentle with the baby. It makes me doubt everything I've ever heard about him. I need to know... Am I falling for an act or...?"

"Or?" Ruth raised her eyebrows. She was smiling a little and seemed to know but wanted Ella to spell it out.

"Or maybe..." Ella worked up to the alternative. "Is it possible that he's not as dangerous as people say? You've said yourself you don't believe a lot of it. It's always vague like, 'I heard he put another girl in the hospital,' or 'It was someone from Genoa this time.' The only real person who's ever been involved is Kathy. That was right after high school, right? That was a long time ago. Maybe he wasn't... I don't know, walking with God then? Or maybe he's had some sort of... And I've heard so many different versions of what happened. Maybe the truth is the least violent. And maybe... maybe I'll think of any excuse I can to believe he wouldn't hurt me because I'm pathetic, and he's cute."

"You're not pathetic," Ruth said.

Ella appreciated the defense. She could tell it was just a reflex, but it was good to have a friend with that reflex.

"Okay. What are you going to do?"

"Ask you for advice."

Ruth smirked. "I don't know what you should do."

"How do I protect myself and still... it would be easier if I knew the truth, if I need to protect myself."

"I wonder what..." Ruth paused. She appeared to be getting an idea.

"You have advice after all?" Ella waited eagerly.

"Well, maybe you need to... *cautiously*... poke the bear."

That odd advice made Ella laugh. "That doesn't help either because I have no idea what you mean."

"You said you wish you knew the truth," Ruth said. "I guess I'm suggesting you ask the one person who can tell you. But carefully."

Ella gasped. "You want me to ask Sebastian what happened with Kathy?"

"I suspect he knows there are different versions floating around and... well, it's possible he'd be... not happy exactly, but maybe relieved to have a chance to tell you the truth about it."

"I... what if he doesn't want to tell me?"

"His reaction might actually be the most valuable information for you. I mean, if he seems remorseful and assures you he's more in control that could be... well, a lot better than if he gets angry or defensive or... A little display of anger might cure you of that crush pretty quickly. But..." Ruth held up a warning finger. "You need to do it when you're not completely alone, just in case."

Ella was terrified of the suggestion, but she was desperate enough to at least hear it out. "Let's say for the sake of argument that I have the guts to ask him," she said. "How am I supposed to find a time when we're alone – because that sounds like a very private conversation – but not completely alone? A restaurant would be a possible setting, public space with separate tables and all. But am I supposed to ask him out to find out if that's a good idea?"

"Yeah, getting to that situation would be a problem." Ruth was looking thoughtful. "Hey, I know. He's been hanging around on Fridays while you wait for me and Gabriel. Maybe I could suggest the four of us go for a late snack, um…" She seemed to be realizing why that wouldn't work.

"You're going to invite us to join you but at a different table?" Ella was amused.

Ruth took it well. "Okay, bad idea. And don't tell him I said this, but I'm not sure Gabriel could take Sebastian if it came to that so he may not be the best protection."

"We need one of those twin black belts," Ella said, more as an observation than a suggestion. Ruth's older brothers were big guys with martial arts training.

"Yes, we do," Ruth said. "That's why Friday is a good starting point. Oh, and I got it this time!" She nodded slowly to herself as though checking for flaws first. "Yes, it's perfect. Sort of. Remember we were just talking a few weeks ago about doing something fun on a Friday instead of a regular meeting? We'll take the whole group somewhere that could…"

"Ice Cream Shack," Ella said. "I know Sebastian likes it because he suggested we go there on Saturday."

"Yeah! They have all those little tables that – Wait! Back up. You saw Sebastian on Saturday?" Ruth's eyes narrowed suspiciously.

"Totally unplanned. I bumped into him on the sidewalk downtown. He was on his way for ice cream and asked if I wanted to go with him."

"He asked you out?"

"No," Ella said. "He was clear that he was just being friendly. But we ended up going to church instead."

"You told me you went to church on Saturday because you told me about Mrs. Donnelly signing you up for the bingo thing. How did you forget to mention that Sebastian was with you when it happened?"

Ella was about to answer when Ruth thought of something else.

"And did you know he was who else would be setting up bingo?"

"Not when I agreed to help," Ella said, "not that I actually agreed to anything."

Ruth didn't appear satisfied by the answer.

"All right. I didn't mention Sebastian on purpose," Ella admitted. "I was afraid something in my voice would give me away. I didn't want to tell you how I felt about him until I had enough time to ask what to do about it."

"How did you go from ice cream to church?"

Ella shrugged. "Totally random. I didn't have any money on me and didn't want to let him pay so he suggested church."

"I hate to say it," Ruth said, "but that is really sweet."

"Don't say that. It wasn't supposed to be sweet. I was congratulating myself on getting out of the ice cream, which might have felt like a date, and then I was sitting in church and realized… oh, yeah, weddings. Mush." Ella mimed melting into a puddle of goo.

"You have it so bad."

"It is so bad," Ella agreed.

"But I think what you're telling me backs up my guess that

you're not the only one. Sounds like he came up with a random idea because he didn't want to miss the opportunity to spend time with you."

Ella grabbed a pen from her desk and threw it at Ruth. "That's still not helping."

"Sorry," Ruth said. She didn't look sorry.

"Let's get back to the plan."

"Right, the plan." Ruth considered. "This Friday, we'll tell everyone that we're meeting at the Ice Cream Shack instead of the church the following Friday. But how do we make sure you and Sebastian are sitting at a table by yourselves?"

Ella shook her head. She had to admit she wasn't thinking very hard though. A big part of her didn't want to make this plan work.

Ruth seemed more determined. "There are a lot of couples in the group now. That might help us guess where certain people will want to sit. But we don't always have exactly the same turnout."

"I noticed the couples," Ella mumbled.

"Okay. I have an idea. Most of the tables have four chairs," Ruth said. "If you and I sit together, Gabriel will come and sit by me, and I'm willing to bet Sebastian will want that other seat by you."

"Maybe not," Ella said, though she found herself hoping that he would. It really wasn't helping.

"Then, once everyone else is sitting down, I'll come up with an excuse for me and Gabriel to join someone else."

"An excuse?"

"Yeah…" Ruth tipped her head side to side. "I'll think of a few things ahead of time I might suddenly want to talk to someone about and find a spot by one of those people."

"What if… never mind."

"What?"

"I was going to ask what if someone suggests pushing the tables together, but they're all attached to the floor there, aren't they?"

"Yeah."

Ella was going over the plan in her mind. "Okay. But what if it doesn't work?"

"If it doesn't work, we still get a treat and to do something different with the group. Win, win."

It wasn't going to work. Ella was fairly sure of that because even if the musical chairs routine panned out, she still had to work up the courage to ask Sebastian something she was very afraid to ask.

4

Sebastian considered himself lucky when the chair next to Ella was available. She always came with Ruth to the Friday night meetings and sat by her. That left only one side open. Sometimes someone else managed to sit there first.

That Friday was a small group though. There were only six people, counting Sebastian and not counting Grace. She definitely counted as a person, but she was too small to take up a chair. "Is Jessica okay?" Sebastian asked Isaac, who was there with his daughter and not his wife.

"Just a bit of a cold," he said.

"I hope she feels better soon," Ruth said.

Isaac nodded appreciation at the concern.

"I can hold her if you need me to," Heather said, eyeing Grace in his arms.

"We're good for now," Isaac replied.

Sebastian admired the way he completely ignored the condescending tone. Heather's offer hadn't sounded as though she particularly wanted to hold the baby but as though Isaac might be incapable of caring for his own child without Jessica's guidance. Then he turned to Ella, "How is everyone else?" He included Ruth in the question so as not to put too much pressure on Ella.

"Good," Ruth said. "We're glad it's Friday though. Right, Ella?"

Ella nodded and said, "Weekend," with a small cheer.

Gabriel opened his notebook, which was the sign that it was time to start. They prayed together before he looked at Ruth.

"First, we've made a decision. Next week will be the fun week. We're going to meet at Ice Cream Shack instead."

"No discussion?" Isaac asked.

"No serious discussion," Ruth said. "We'll all just hang out." Heather nodded.

Sebastian said he thought that sounded good.

"Oh, I get it," Isaac said. "You two just want a break from having to plan anything."

There was some chuckling at the sibling teasing.

"We are planning," Ruth said. "We're planning ice cream."

"Oh, that's hard," Isaac said. "Are you also buying the ice cream?"

"No." Ruth smiled at her brother with fake sweetness. "We were planning on you buying the ice cream."

Isaac laughed. He wasn't alone. Ella enjoyed the banter.

"We're missing a few people though," Gabriel said. "I'll stop here on the way to post a note on the door to redirect anyone who comes here first or might forget." He looked around as people nodded agreement. "So that's the plan for next week. This week we're talking about St. Francis. He came from a rich family but chose to give up everything for God. He owned nothing but the clothes on his back. He lived on the street and begged for food. His preaching that God was the only thing people really needed eventually got enough of a following to form an entire religious order." He nudged Ruth.

"We thought we could use him to start a discussion about materialism, charitable giving, and how much is too much, that sort of thing." Ruth read from something on her phone screen. "I think we can say God doesn't expect all of us to give up everything, but we still –"

"It's amazing when you think about it," Heather interrupted, "that some homeless beggar got a bunch of people to follow him around. That wouldn't happen today. Can you imagine Jojo with an entourage?" She laughed mockingly.

"Jojo isn't homeless," Sebastian said. That was a popular misconception around town that irked him. Not because there was necessarily anything shameful about being homeless but because it was unjust to the woman who made sure he wasn't.

"Really?" Heather asked.

Gabriel shook his head. "He lives next door to me actually."

"Do you know Mrs. Johnson, the woman who owns Granny's Shelf?"

"I've never been in there," Heather said.

"Well, she's his sister," Sebastian explained. "And his legal guardian. She pays his rent, buys his groceries, and takes care of all his finances."

"Then why does he go around begging?"

"He doesn't," Sebastian said. "Some of the restaurants give him food because he doesn't understand money. Mrs. Johnson tried to set up accounts where people record what they give him so she can pay for it later, but most refused."

"Still amazing that St. Francis gathered a following as a homeless man," Heather said.

"He must have been a good speaker," Ella observed.

Sebastian nodded at her. He was happy to keep the conversation on St. Francis. And happy that her speaking up gave him an excuse to look at her. She was wearing green glasses that matched her shirt and her hair was curly.

"He must have been good at explaining detachment," Isaac

said. "I think that's the primary principle, that we don't have to give up everything as long as we *could*. Could we give up everything we owned to, for example, save the life of someone we love."

"Easier said than done," Heather said.

"What do you mean?" Gabriel asked her.

"Well, I think most people would quickly say they would, but... if you really think about how hard it would be to live in poverty for the rest of your life..." Heather tilted her head and didn't appear to know exactly how she wanted to finish. "If it would be hard, does that mean you weren't properly detached from your possessions?"

"I'm not sure it's fair to..."

All heads turned to Ruth as she tried to put her thoughts into words.

"If some guy came up to you and, let's say, your mom on the street," Ruth said, "and said he'd kill her if you didn't hand over everything in your pockets... We'd all do it, and in that case it'd be easy. But it's difficult to imagine a situation where you could really trade abject poverty for someone's life."

"Medical bills can add up," Isaac said.

"True," Gabriel said. "But there's rarely a guarantee that medicine can save a life and each case would be a little different. Would you drain your savings to treat your mother if it meant you might have to watch your children starve?"

"That's really not fair," Ruth said. "Let's not talk about giving up *everything*, but... How do you make sure you're not falling into greed? When do you know you have too much stuff?"

"That might be a question for Grace," Isaac said. "I swear our house exploded with stuff after she was born."

Ruth playfully reprimanded her brother. "*She* didn't buy any of it, did she?"

"No," he acknowledged. "I know we have more than we need, but I don't know how to… to decide. Hopefully, we'll have it figured out by the second kid."

"It's hard because…" Ella started quietly, then she raised her voice to be heard. "It's hard because we do need some things."

"We're not supposed to need anything but God," Heather said.

"But we do." Ella turned slightly pink but kept trying to make her point. "We need food. God wants us to value our own lives enough to take care of ourselves. We just don't need to have our favorite food every day."

"That's why so many people struggle with dieting," Sebastian said. "You can't just quit food cold turkey. You have to figure out how much is too much. People have a legitimate need for shelter, too. But does one person need a four-thousand-square-foot house?"

"Need? No," Ruth said. "But is it necessarily wrong?"

"Depends on a lot of things." Isaac turned his fussing baby around and made faces at her while he talked. "Is this man shackling himself with a debt he'll never repay to have the giant house? Does he really enjoy the extra space because he has relatives who visit a lot or does he have a huge house only to impress others?"

"So you're saying motivation is important?" Gabriel asked.

"That's definitely a factor."

Ruth said, "I don't think we're talking about detachment anymore."

"I think you changed the subject," Heather said.

"Did I?"

Isaac smiled at his sister over Grace's head. "You moved us on to greed."

"Oh." Ruth gave Ella a self-deprecating smile.

Then Ella turned to Sebastian to share the amusement. It was only a quick smile with eye contact, but it was only for him and was very distracting. When his mind returned to the discussion, Gabriel was talking about how he liked to invent hamburgers, which made no sense and definitely didn't have anything to do with detachment or greed.

Emily and Joseph arrived, slightly late as usual. That was expected because Emily didn't get off work until eight. Everyone had assured her it was okay to come when she could. The discussion continued much as it started, with people turning everything into a complicated example of when too much was too much. It probably wasn't the most productive meeting they'd ever had but still interesting. They met in the teachers lounge of the school and had to put the room back the way the teachers kept it when they were done. Between Fridays and bingo, Sebastian spent an unusual amount of time moving chairs.

He managed to time his exit to coincide with Ella's. It worked that if he walked out with her, she would stop to chat while Ruth and Gabriel said their goodbyes. Ella took a place off to the side as they exited the building, pretending to read a bulletin board on the outside wall. Ruth had pulled Gabriel to the other side of the doors. She glanced at Sebastian before she stepped a bit closer to Gabriel. There was something in her demeanor that seemed more conspiratorial than intimate.

Sebastian shrugged off that impression. It wasn't any of his business, and he didn't care anyway. As long as those two were keeping each other busy, he could talk to Ella. "Hey, Ella," he said. "Did you enjoy tonight's meeting?"

"Yeah. Ruth is funny when Isaac is goading her."

"I know. I –"

"Ella!" Ruth called. "It's so nice out. I'm going to walk to Mrs. Donnelly's with Gabriel, then I'll come right back for you." She slipped her hand into Gabriel's as she spoke and had already taken a few backwards steps before she finished.

Ella said nothing in response. She was looking after her friend with a rather stunned expression on her face. It was cute. Her eyes darted to Sebastian, to the parking lot, back to Ruth and Gabriel disappearing around the front of the church, and finally landed somewhere near Sebastian's shoulder. "I guess I know what Ruth and I will be talking about on the way home," she said.

Sebastian felt a short laugh escape at her tone, but the words made him curious. There were a few things he knew. He knew Ella got a ride to and from the Friday meetings with Ruth. He knew Gabriel dropped a key to the building at Mrs. Donnelly's house on his way home.

Ruth must know the sudden change of plans would give him a longer than usual time alone with Ella, which seemed to indicate that she trusted him to be alone with Ella. At least as far as standing on the edge of a well-lit parking lot counted as alone. Would this vote of confidence help him win Ella over? She sounded as though she was looking forward to giving Ruth a hard time but not as though she was truly upset at being left. "How is this conversation going to begin?" he asked.

Ella sighed. "Well, I usually prefer to be consulted before I'm abandoned."

"What would you have said if she asked?" He immediately regretted the question because it put Ella on the spot to admit she didn't mind being left with him or gave her an opportunity to say she did mind. "You're not really abandoned anyway since…" Okay, that was worse. In his haste to keep Ella from saying something he didn't want to hear, he was about to point out that she could easily walk home. He might as well say goodbye. He turned to a picture on the bulletin board for help. "Looks like the fifth graders had fun at the May crowning."

Ella nodded. She could see the smiling faces as well as he could.

"You went to elementary school here, didn't you? You probably did that when you were here."

"Yeah." Ella looked at the sidewalk.

"I think I'm failing at entertaining you during this abandonment."

Her lips twitched with a possibility of a smile. "Are you trying to entertain me?"

"Well, I'm mostly thinking of Ruth," he said. "The more frustrated you are at having to wait, the more you're going to yell at her."

"Oh." She smiled faintly without looking up. "So you, um... plan to stick around until she gets back?"

That sounded like a hint. Was it a hint that she wanted him to stay or that she wanted him to go away? "Unless you don't want me to distract you. Would you rather stand around getting mad at Ruth?"

"I, um... How long do you think she'll be gone?"

Sebastian slipped his phone halfway from his pocket to check the time. The current time had nothing to do with how long it might take to walk to Mrs. Donnelly's house and back. He wanted an excuse to look down, to cover the disappointment that Ella had answered without saying whether she wanted him to wait with her or not. "I bet she'll be back before ten."

"Why do you... never mind." Ella turned to watch a car pass through the parking lot, presumably more to hide a growing blush than from interest in the car. But there had been a glimmer of interest that Sebastian couldn't let go.

"Why do I what?" he asked.

"Nothing." Her eyes flicked to the pocket where he'd put the phone though.

There was a question he'd gotten enough to make it a reasonable guess. He pulled the phone all the way out and flipped it open. "Why do I have this incredibly lame flip phone and not a real one?"

Ella began to shake her head before she stopped herself and said, "Well, yeah. I know you used to have a better phone. What made you downgrade?"

Most people got a dismissive answer about it being a personal preference. Ella wasn't most people. He had to be completely open so she'd believe him when they finally addressed the rumors of violence that surrounded him. "I've mentioned before how I'm careful about anything that might lead to addiction. The family history makes me worry I could be more susceptible. People talk about smartphone addiction, but I used to ignore that as not a real… Then, a little before Christmas, I thought I lost my phone. It turned up in the pocket of a coat I don't wear often, but… I just had this awful panic while it was missing. It made me realize I might actually be too attached to it. Switching to this one," he folded it up and put it away, "was so hard it kind of confirmed I made the right call. The first few weeks, I was constantly trying to check stuff, and I didn't even know what I wanted to check half the time. It was like a compulsion to look for something to look at. I'm glad to be rid of it now."

"Really?" Ella raised her eyebrows skeptically. "I mean, I definitely respect your decision to steer clear of addiction, but there's nothing you miss?"

"You got me," he said. He'd sounded less than earnest and

wondered if she'd question it. "I can say I'm glad to be rid of it… most of the time. I'm more relaxed, and it's really weird but I'm not worried about missing something when I'm not constantly being notified of things. On the other hand, this thing is a pain to text with, and I had to borrow my mom's GPS a while back and… I've been tentatively planning to keep the lame phone for a full year, for a clean slate, then go back to a smartphone but be much more intentional about how I use it so I'm in control and not the other way around."

Ella nodded at him. "Sounds like a good idea. You say your mom has one? It's not… I mean, she doesn't…"

"It isn't a problem for her. She mostly uses it as a phone and occasionally to point out how *other people* use it to share pictures of their grandkids."

"She'd get along with my… oh." Ella's expression shifted from exasperated to embarrassed. "But you meant, um… I'm sorry she doesn't have pictures of her grandkids."

"Oh, don't… ach." Sebastian panicked at the direction of the conversation. He'd started kicking himself for bringing up his mom's hints for grandchildren in front of Ella, afraid she might read some of his hopes when he looked at her and suddenly decide she needed to walk home after all. But then she'd laughed and began to commiserate until she misinterpreted the comment as his mom mourning her lack of pictures from her older sons.

Ella was standing there looking uncomfortable for the wrong reason and bringing her back to another reason wasn't going to fix anything. He needed to clear things up and move on quickly. "Don't worry," he said. "You were right that when my mom comments on grandkids she means to… they're directed at me, but, um… let's talk about something else." Maybe they could talk about how that was the most eloquent subject change ever.

Ella mashed her lips together rather than laugh at it. Then her face softened. "Can I... ask you something?"

"Yes."

"It's, uh... kind of..." Her eyes studied the sidewalk as she searched for the words.

It was clearly a question that made her nervous. A lot of questions made her nervous, but could this be it? Was she going to ask if the rumors were true? Sebastian wanted to assure her that she could ask anything. He held his tongue lest assurance sound like pushiness.

"When did you know?" she asked abruptly.

"I want to answer, but I don't understand the question."

Ella sort of rolled her eyes at herself and took a big breath. "About your mom being an alcoholic and her former family," she said. "It sounds like she's been very honest about everything with you, but it's not something you can explain to a two-year-old and I... wondered... Was it hard when you found out?"

"Oh." Sebastian found himself fighting a smile as he absorbed the question. Grinning over a serious subject would be highly inappropriate. It was a real question though. It was a sign that Ella wasn't just passing the time, a sign that she might be beginning to care.

Sebastian's mom had lost custody of two small boys when she was drinking and hadn't seen or spoken to either of them since. She'd made overtures a few times over the years and gotten no response. One of them, Steve, had sent Christmas cards the last two years. They were printed cards that Sebastian's mom suspected were actually mailed by Steve's wife. She didn't reply to the cards for fear the woman would be asked to stop sending them. The pictures of his family were treasures. Most of the time though, his mom didn't mention her lost boys and seemed to accept that they were happy without her.

"I'm not sure exactly," he said, thinking back as he spoke. "I think my mom must have done a good job of telling me gradually as I was able to understand. There's always been a picture in our living room of her with two small boys who I knew were my brothers. I think when I was really little, I assumed they had died because she'd said my dad died. But I also remember her saying she couldn't take care of them because she had been sick without giving details. By the time I got to middle school, I somehow already knew what classmates meant when they called me the drunk's mistake."

Ella winced at the insult.

He kept talking. He didn't want to give her time to pity him over old slurs that didn't matter. "Most of her story just came out naturally over time. I only remember one sort of big conversation. I must have been maybe fifteen or sixteen and she sat me down to talk about how I was getting to the age people might start offering me drinks at parties and how I needed to always keep in mind that it might affect me differently than some people. She said... well, she got pretty emotional talking about the possibility of me making some of the same mistakes she did and..." Sebastian waved off the depressing memories. "I wasn't cool enough to get invited to those parties anyway."

A tiny laugh of surprise found his ears before Ella bit her lip to suppress it. She was looking at him and not the sidewalk. The eye contact wasn't steady but bouncing back and forth between tracing his jaw and hairline and seemed to be studying his expression for whatever it could add to his words. Maybe it was his imagination. For a moment though, he saw something that looked like admiration. It triggered a primal force in his chest that wanted to jump out and pull Ella close, to kiss her, hold her, and never let go.

It was actually a terrifying thought, mostly because of how much it would terrify Ella to know it existed. Sebastian restrained himself so forcefully he took a step backwards. Lighter conversation was a must. "When was the last party *you* went to?"

Her face revealed how unexpected the question was as she shrugged. "I don't know. I think I went to someone's birthday party in third grade."

He shook his head. "That's not the last party you went to."

"How do you know?" she said, sounding more sad than defensive.

"Hey. Don't you go with Ruth to her parents' house almost every Sunday?"

"What does that have to do with anything?"

"There are a bunch of people there," he said. "That's a party."

She rewarded him with a pretty smile that was relaxed enough to stick around. "No, it isn't."

"Only her parents live there, right? Everyone else comes in response to an invitation?"

"Sort of."

"A verbal invitation?"

She nodded reluctantly.

"And then you all eat together. That's a dinner party."

"It's lunch," she said, still smiling.

"So it's a casual party. It's still a party."

Ella sighed as she conceded his point. "Actually, I need to thank Emily for, um…" She trailed off as though she fully expected Sebastian to ignore the fact that she'd started to say something.

"Thank her for what?" he prompted.

"Oh, um... Once Emily started coming with Joseph, I was the only one not part of a couple, and I tried to bow out but Ruth was insistent that I had to keep coming because her mom would be offended if I didn't and... that's nonsense. The woman has thicker skin than that. Anyway, Emily decided that Ruth and I should go to her place after we eat and Heather and Julia join us." She nodded towards the school to indicate she meant the Heather and Julia he knew from the young adult group. "So now it's like free food and then games with a few friends instead of lunch followed by the awkward discussion of which games we can play with an odd number of players where everyone tries not to look at me as the odd person."

Ella narrowed her eyes as she finished talking. It appeared to Sebastian as though she was daring him to call her odd. It was tempting to point out how she'd left herself open to that teasing.

"You're about to say that I *am* odd, aren't you?" she accused.

"Don't put words in my mouth."

"I didn't put them in your head."

"Odd just means different, which isn't necessarily a bad thing."

"And there it is!" Ella held her hands out like she was displaying a large sign. "That was you admitting that you were thinking I'm odd."

"I don't... uh..." Had he said that? At this point, Sebastian was wondering if Ella had put the words in his head. This non-timid version of her was wonderful but also a bit scary. He wasn't entirely sure she wasn't offended. Was he screwing this up?

And then she lowered her hands and started laughing. "It's okay," she said. "I'm only odd sometimes."

Sebastian smiled and tried to hold his head steady so nothing could be perceived as agreement. Though on the inside, he was thinking how much he liked odd sometimes.

"When was the last time you went to a party?" Ella asked.

"Well…" Sebastian gave the question a moment's thought. Since they'd already established a fairly loose definition of party, he knew what he had to say. "I recently had the pleasure of attending an event where I was the only male guest and the only one not over seventy."

Ella pinched her lips and let out a quick snort. "Care to explain how you ended up at a party for old women?"

"My mom is part of a weekly card club. I think she's actually one of the younger women. I always drive her, and I made the mistake of escorting her inside rather than simply dropping her off." It had been shortly after his mom got her walker. He had thought perhaps if he showed it to her friends, they might be more successful in talking her into using it.

"Why was that a mistake?"

"Because I got invited to stay," Sebastian said. "Aggressively invited."

"Aggressively invited?" Now Ella was laughing with him instead of at him. She may not have been laughing at him before, but this was still better.

"Yeah. Evelyn Johnson was hosting. She asked me to stay and cheer on my mom. I thought she was kidding so I just smiled and turned to leave. But Ellen had moved in front of the door, and she insisted it would be great to have me because they were going to be missing at least one woman."

"What do they play?" Ella asked when he paused.

"It varies. I think it's been pinochle for a while."

"Do you know how to play?"

"Yes and no. That's why I was afraid they were trying to get me to fill in."

Ella tipped her head and raised questioning eyes to his to show she wanted more information.

"I know the basics, but you have never met a more competitive group. They insist on total silence once the hand is dealt because no one wants to be distracted and a few of them are paranoid about kibitzing. Then once the hand is over, anyone who misplayed is gonna hear about it."

Ella nodded that she understood his reluctance to join a game that serious.

"I think that's how they got me," he said. "Several ladies surrounded me to block the exit and when I realized they were only asking me to watch with whoever was sitting out, I was relieved enough to agree before I considered how much fun that would be."

"It might be fun to watch a little," Ella said. "Was it a long night?"

"It didn't start out too bad. My mom drew one of the short straws, so to speak. They actually have this complicated system of drawing cards to match up the teams and… Anyway, she and Mrs. Johnson were the first two to sit out. You know Mrs. Johnson from Granny's Shelf."

"Sort of," Ella said. "I've only been in there the one time."

Sebastian clearly remembered the one time. Apparently, he'd been even luckier than he thought to bump into her there. Although he still wondered if she'd seen him coming or if she'd really been interested in that bunny. "She's pretty nice and makes an awesome apple walnut pie, which she brought out for the three of us to enjoy while we watched the first game. We had a quiet chat when we weren't being shushed for an important trick. But then there was some shuffling for the second round."

He paused for a moment to figure out how to word what had happened. He didn't want to sound as though he was making a bid for sympathy or as though he was hiding something. "I was joined by two ladies who were less interested in my company. One just pulled her chair a bit farther away and acted hyper-focused on the cards. The other was kind of glaring at me in between weirdly suspicious glances at my mom, as though it was her fault I was there. My mom was one of the least insistent that I stay and did not protest when I slipped out with a reminder that she should text me for a ride when they were wrapping up."

"Sounds like you were a little out of place." Ella's tone said she knew that was an understatement.

"Yes," he said.

"But you got pie out of it so…" She raised her eyebrows and appeared to suggest he might make that deal again.

He might. But this time with Ella was so much better than pie, and it was almost over. Ruth was approaching.

"Looks like my ride is back," Ella said. She gave a quick wave before she dashed off to meet Ruth halfway.

Sebastian walked towards his car with less enthusiasm.

5

Ella sent Ruth a punishing glare. "What was that!?" she hissed.

Ruth might have been trying to convey innocence or confusion with her smile, but mostly she showed how unaffected she was by the glare. "What was what?"

Ella answered only by continuing to glower. She wanted to wait until they were safely inside Ruth's car in case some of their words might carry in the stillness of the night. Once the doors were closed, she let loose on her friend. "Why did you leave me alone with Sebastian?"

"I didn't," Ruth said. "I just went for a walk with Gabriel. I didn't know Sebastian was going to wait with you." She glanced up at Ella as she buckled her seat belt.

"If you're checking to see if I'm buying your innocent act..." Ella finished with a stern shake of her head.

Long red hair flipped over Ruth's shoulder as she looked behind her before backing up. And she laughed. "Okay, I didn't know he'd stay, but I thought he might. I think that confirms my suspicions." She wiggled her eyebrows.

"What about the plan?" Ella asked.

"The plan?"

"Uh, yeah. The plan where I get a table with Sebastian next week to ask about Kathy."

"I remember the plan," Ruth said. "It was my brilliant idea, after all." The smugness in her voice was joking.

"What just happened was *not* part of the plan."

"It was a last-minute addition." Ruth flashed a smile, then got more serious. "I really was trying to help. I know you're afraid of not having enough courage to ask him what really happened so I thought maybe a little more time together would help you be more comfortable."

Ella put her hands over her face. She was yelling at Ruth, but she was really upset with herself. They both knew it. "It was awful," she said. "I was telling him about how odd I am and trying to get him to agree and I don't even know what that was. Meanwhile, he told me this funny story about how he got sucked into watching his mom's friends play cards, and I was smiling at him like some sort of dope."

"I'm sure it wasn't as bad as you think." Ruth sounded thoughtful. "I mean, did you notice how he was watching you walk away?"

"No. I was trying very hard not to look."

"He was disappointed you were leaving."

Ella groaned. "Why are you encouraging me? The whole reason for the plan was to figure out if I should be worried about getting involved with him. You shouldn't be leaving me alone with him yet."

Ruth opened her mouth but didn't say anything. She seemed to be processing some thoughts. Eventually, she said, "First of all, you were out in public, not really alone. Second of all, I wasn't worried. I don't... I don't think it's fair to say I want to trust him just because my brother does either. While it's true that I've hardly ever spoken to Sebastian outside of Friday nights, we've had a lot of Friday nights. Everything he says sounds completely earnest. He's disagreed with people without ever raising his voice. I... I don't think I'm being naïve not to worry."

"Are you saying you don't think I even need to ask him now?"

"No." Ruth shook her head. "I think it's important that you find out the truth. If there is violence in his past, you deserve to know what steps he's taken to keep it there, how it might affect a relationship and so on. And if there isn't, he deserves a chance to tell you that."

Ella nodded. She agreed that the question was important. Sebastian had to know that she'd been told at least some things about him that weren't true. Their relationship would have a pretty shaky foundation if it appeared she didn't care where the line was between fact and fiction. But she knew tracing that line would be hard.

****

Ella was in Ruth's car again late Sunday morning. She and Gabriel usually rode with Ruth to her parents' house after church. Getting to that usual point had a usual path for Gabriel. He lived next door to the church and walked regardless of the weather. He also dressed up every day, except when he was out running, and didn't feel a need to stop at home to take off his tie or anything else.

It was a bit more complicated for Ella. She lived close enough to walk to church if the weather was nice and she wasn't wearing the pretty shoes with the ridiculous heels. But her parents always drove so sometimes she got a ride with them. Sometimes she wanted to change into more comfortable clothes after church and sometimes not. She didn't like to be too casual for visiting.

Most weeks, Ella made a plan and then exchanged a few texts with Ruth about whether she should wait for her after church or go to Ella's house to pick her up.

That Sunday she was happy she planned to leave with Ruth. It made her exit a lot easier. She was sitting with her parents a few pews behind Sebastian and his mom. Ella was proud of herself for not making a big deal of the proximity. They both noticed her as they turned around to leave. She gave a big, friendly smile and returned the nod of greeting before rushing over to Ruth, who was clearly waiting for her. It didn't look as though she was trying to avoid a conversation with the younger or older Jones. It wasn't that she didn't want to talk to them anyway. She was just sure she'd say something to embarrass herself if she did.

Ella climbed into the backseat to let Gabriel and his longer legs sit next to Ruth. He'd given up offering to switch with her. Ella didn't need to stop home to change, but Ruth did. Though it wasn't exactly an extra stop.

"I'm going to change in case I can get in a game before we head to Emily's," Ruth said as she parked next to her parents' house. There was a basketball hoop in the driveway. Ruth lived in a tiny apartment in the backyard.

Gabriel nodded. "I'll see if I can help with lunch." He walked towards the Zieberts' back door while Ella followed Ruth to her front door.

There was a small kitchen where they entered. A table with two chairs was pushed into a corner. Ella didn't bother sitting as she knew Ruth would be fast. Ruth slipped into her bedroom wearing a dress and sandals and returned in shorts, sneakers and a sweatshirt still pulling her hair into a ponytail. "Let's go," she said.

Ella opened the door.

They met Isaac and Jessica as they arrived.

"You look ready to lose, Baby Ruth," Isaac said, nodding towards the basketball hoop.

"Good morning, Jessica," Ruth said, pointedly ignoring her brother. This wasn't because of the taunting but because of the nickname. "Grace make it through church this morning?"

The six-month-old was asleep in her car seat.

"Rough start," Jessica said, "but then it was time for a nap."

Isaac opened the screen door for the three women.

Ella mumbled a thank you as she passed the tall muscular man. He shared Ruth's coloring, though his hair was almost too short to tell its color, and would have been very intimidating if he didn't also share her friendly personality. He let the door close rather than follow the others inside as another car parked by the house. That would be Joseph and Emily.

The kitchen had a warm savory smell. Gabriel had been put to work chopping an onion. Mrs. Ziebert swooped towards the baby carrier and froze with a frown, presumably in response to the closed eyes. Then she turned towards Ruth and Ella. "I wanted to sprinkle some cheese on the quiche as it comes out of the oven, and I don't have as much as I thought," she said. "Would you girls be willing to run to Seymour's for me?"

"Sure," Ruth said.

Mrs. Ziebert reached for a purse on a hook. "One bag of shredded Parmesan."

"I can afford cheese, Mom." Ruth turned and motioned Ella back to the door.

Ella squinted as she stepped outside yet again. She wished for a moment that she'd worn her red glasses that darkened in the sun, but she thought the pink paisley blouse had enough color and chose the silver frames instead. The sound of dribbling met her ears as her eyes adjusted. Ruth's brothers had already gotten out a ball.

Ruth pointed at them. "If lunch isn't ready when I get back, I want in."

"Where are you going?" Joseph asked.

"Errand for Mom."

"Hey, I'll come." Emily jumped up from where she was sitting on the edge of the driveway.

Ella had been about to open the passenger door and moved to the back door to make room for Emily.

Emily noticed and ran around to the other side of the car. "We'll make Ruth sit in front alone like a chauffeur." She climbed in next to Ella and added, "Where are we going?"

"Seymour's."

"Oh, missing ingredient." Emily nodded. "I'm surprised that happened to Joanna. She's so organized and everything. She's going to make our wedding cake, you know."

Ella smiled. "July 2nd. That's only like five or six weeks away, right?"

"Five weeks and five days. Or four days? Maybe it's four weeks." Emily appeared unconcerned by her uncertainty. "It's close anyway," she said. "My mom is freaking out that I don't have a dress yet. She actually took Tuesday morning off work to go shopping with me. Julia said she'd come with me on Wednesday if we don't find anything so hopefully I can remind my mom of the backup if she seems too tightly wound. She keeps asking me what I'm looking for and then claims I'm contradicting myself. I want lace but no beads or sequins or anything shiny and those are different things so... long but not..." She suddenly grabbed the back of Ruth's seat. "Have you talked to Adam?"

Ella kind of felt like *she* needed to take a breath after that answer. She liked Emily, but sometimes the confidence behind her stream-of-consciousness style of conversation was a bit overwhelming. There was also a pang for Ruth, who hadn't told anyone else how much she struggled not to be envious that she wasn't also planning a wedding. Emily had jumped right from that subject to asking about her estranged brother.

Ruth only shook her head.

"We're mailing out the invitations this week," Emily said. "Joseph is afraid that Adam won't come and that he'll regret it… that it'll make it even harder to restart communication after a snub like that. But he won't talk to him first. He's like he's getting an invitation and then it's on him. But what if a wedding is too big, too much pressure to show up? I think he should text him about how his day is going or something simple to… Joseph talked to Mrs. Donnelly this morning."

The sudden shift made Ella physically jump.

Even from the side it was clear that Ruth was amused. "Really?" she asked. "What is he signed up for now?"

"Nothing yet."

Ruth gasped playfully. "He actually said no to Mrs. Donnelly?"

"Not exactly. He told her maybe."

"Oh. That's just a delayed yes," Ruth said.

"That's what Joseph said." Emily looked at Ella to make sure she was included even though she wasn't speaking. "I brought it up because she asked him to be a reader at Mass. She was saying how he has a perfect voice for it, and I do love his voice. It's deep and sexy and –"

"Family member in the car," Ruth interrupted.

Ella and Emily both laughed. Ruth considered it a great misfortune to have three attractive brothers and preferred that no one comment on how they looked in her presence. That apparently applied to how they sounded as well.

"Anyway," Emily said, "Mrs. Donnelly mentioned that she was working on Adam for the same ministry. It seems he's been coming to the Saturday Masses regularly. I think that's a great sign. Joseph said he stopped going to church long before he stopped talking to the family so maybe if he's coming back to one he's almost ready to come back to the other. But obviously it's not my place to get involved. I just have to watch Joseph stubbornly refuse to talk to Adam first, while claiming he's respecting his wish to be left alone, and pray that it works out anyway." She sighed and unbuckled her seat belt as she opened her door. They had arrived at Seymour's while she was talking.

Ella got out as well and joined the others.

"Wait a sec, guys." Ruth stopped them before they walked towards the store. "I have an idea." She had pulled out her phone and was staring at the still dark screen. She nodded as though making up her mind and began to tap on the screen as she talked. "I'm going to invite Adam to meet with the group this Friday. It's not just a family thing and... Well, it's gonna be more casual than usual so... Our Friday church group is meeting at Ice Cream Shack this week for a break. Think about joining us, okay?" She paused. Blew out a nervous breath. "Send," she said, then motioned Emily and Ella to start walking. "I haven't texted him in months since he ignored so many. I suppose it won't hurt anything if he ignores one more and maybe..." She shrugged but did look a bit hopeful.

The grocery store wasn't called Seymour's anymore. It had the name long enough that locals still used it. The doors rumbled as they slid open. Emily turned to Ruth as she stepped inside. "What are we here for?"

"Cheese," Ruth said.

The three women walked in silence to the refrigerated aisle. It wasn't a particularly large store. They were soon standing in front of a cooler scanning bags of shredded cheese. While Ruth grabbed what would complete the mission, Ella moved out of the way of a woman pushing a shopping cart. She locked eyes with Ella for a moment, and there was a click of recognition. Rather than wave or say hello, she turned to the man next to her and began to whisper as they passed. The man glanced over his shoulder at Ella a minute later. They were talking about her. Why were they talking about her?

Ella felt her face flush. She smoothed a hand over her hair as she checked that her blouse was buttoned and her shoes matched.

"Are you okay?" Ruth asked.

"Yeah. Um, yeah. Let's go." Ella gestured towards the front of the store and followed her friends still feeling very self-conscious.

Only two checkout lanes were open. Ruth got in the shorter line even though Maria was at that register, which was probably why the line was shorter. The woman had dark hair streaked with gray and a comment about too many of the items set in front of her. They were friendly, well-meaning comments but in a voice that carried to everyone in the vicinity. Ella preferred not to have her purchases broadcast. Maria couldn't have much to say about one bag of cheese though. Ella settled in for a short wait.

The only customer ahead of them was a woman Ella vaguely recognized from high school. She thought her name was Amelia but couldn't remember if she'd been one or two years ahead of her. She had a cart full of groceries and a baby in the seat. Emily was making faces at the baby to get him to smile at her. Maria was pausing every few items to ask a stream of questions. How many pears are in here? Do you like this brand of peanut butter? Did you notice that the regular size of this cereal is on sale this week and cheaper per ounce than the larger size? Have you tried the organic peppers?

Amelia answered each question with a one-word answer about a quarter of the volume it'd been asked. She might have been legitimately distracted by the squeals of delight Emily was pulling from her child.

Finally, Maria picked up the Parmesan. Rather than scan it, she began a guessing game with Ruth. "Spaghetti?" she asked.

"No."

"Lasagna?"

"No."

"Pizza?"

"No."

"Omelet?"

"Close," Ruth said. "Quiche."

Ella wasn't sure how that counted as close, but the answer prompted Maria to ring up the cheese. Ruth swiped her card and it seemed they were about to be on their way. Ella was the last of the three women to move out of the line though. Maria caught her eye before she could leave and said, "I hope you know what you're doing."

Too stunned and confused to respond, Ella just stared at her. Maria turned to the next customer without waiting for her to recover. Ella started walking away in a daze.

"What was that all about?" Ruth asked her.

"I don't know."

Both Ruth and Emily shrugged and continued towards the exit. Ella continued to puzzle over the comment as she walked. The meaning hit her at the same moment as the sun. "Sebastian," she whispered.

"What?" Ruth asked.

Emily turned to look across the parking lot as though he might be walking towards them.

"People think I'm dating Sebastian," Ella said. "That's why people are talking about me."

"Are you?" Emily asked.

"No!" Ella shook her head adamantly, trying to stop the blush from rising on her cheeks. She was afraid the next question would be whether or not she wanted to be dating him.

Emily didn't ask though. She smiled sympathetically. "I'm sorry. I'd go back in there and tell her she's misinformed if I thought it would do any good."

"I don't want people talking about me even if it's true," Ella said, though she did appreciate Emily's sentiment.

Ruth nodded. "I assume you'd like us to change the subject if Heather or Julia asks about something they've heard? Well, if Heather asks."

"Yes, please," Ella said.

"If Heather brings up Sebastian at all," Emily said, "I'll simply ask her when she plans to visit me at work next."

"She visits you at work?" Ruth looked at Ella to confirm she'd been about to ask the same thing.

"I'm not gossiping," Emily said. "I'm just relating a few facts. And the fact is, Heather has come to see me at Burger Brothers several times over the last few weeks, and somehow she always ends up spending a lot more time talking to Luke than to me."

6

Sebastian's mom looked up from her puzzle with a sly smile. "What's a four-letter word for pretty?"

He wasn't going to play. He turned on the water to rinse the pan he'd been washing and to drown out whatever her next clue might be. It would also have nothing to do with the puzzle sitting in front of her on the kitchen table.

Soft laughter trailed off as the last of the water ran down the drain. Sebastian didn't know what was funny about being ignored, but he wasn't going to ask. She'd probably think that was funny, too. He set the pan on the drying rack and turned to face his mom. "We'll need to go soon," he said. It was almost time to set up for bingo, almost time to see Ella. He didn't need his mom's taunting clues to think of her.

"In a few minutes," she said. "What makes you so eager?"

"It's called being on time. We'll need to allow for you walking slowly if you plan on refusing the walker."

She sent the thing a dirty look. "I'll walk the exact speed I walked the week before Ella got signed up to help." She smiled somewhat smugly, then it fell away. "And by the way, I'm still capable of folding my own clothes."

"You're capable of folding them while sitting on the bench, too," Sebastian said. "Why do you insist on walking back and forth between the basket and the dresser for each item?"

"It's three steps, and I don't have much chance for exercise in this house. Would you prefer I lie in bed all day like an invalid?"

Sebastian stopped himself from rolling his eyes. His mom always went to a dramatic extreme when he suggested she be careful. But this was the first time he detected a hint of fear in her voice. "If you use the walker, you could get even more exercise. You'd have to constantly move it out of your way and some of the clothes would come unfolded when you drape them over the handles so you'd have to refold them and…" He stopped talking when he saw her chest shaking against the laugh she was trying to hide.

She drew in a steadying breath and said, "What's your plan?"

"Uh… what plan?"

"You don't have a plan?"

"I don't even know what you're talking about."

She rolled her eyes at him. "The situation is worse than I thought." Her eyes dropped to her puzzle a second before she said, "A nine-letter word for a man who will be single forever?"

Oh, great. She was trying to talk about Ella again. "Do you want a sweater for bingo tonight?"

"You need to tell her that you want to spend more time with her. She can't agree to something you don't ask."

"I asked if you want me to get you a sweater."

His mom stared at him. The wrinkles around her eyes got more pronounced as she tried to reinforce her point by leaving it dangling. She reached up and felt the fabric of her short sleeve, pausing a moment to examine a bruise it only partially covered. After a few moments, she said, "I'll take the navy one. I believe that one ended up on top after I fixed your pathetic attempt at folding."

Sebastian left her muttering about how she knew she'd taught him better to get the sweater from her room. When he returned, she looked past the sweater to study the shirt he was wearing. "I suppose you're lucky someone invented permanent press."

"It's been months, Mom," he said, shaking his head. "I don't feel guilty and if you keep trying to make me, someone's going to think you have an unhealthy obsession with laundry."

She shoved her puzzle book aside as she prepared to shove herself from her seat. "Locked me out of my own basement and doesn't feel guilty," she said.

He'd put a lock on the door to keep her from trying to do laundry when he wasn't home. She'd been dropping reminders of her displeasure every chance she got since. He wondered if making him have the same conversation over and over was her way of feeling less helpless. He'd taken away her power to wash her own clothes, but she still had the power to never let him forget it.

"Could have put up a handrail," she said. She took the sweater he offered and moved around the walker towards the front door.

The steps to the basement would still have been narrow and steep. He'd given serious thought to hiring someone to install hookups for the washer and dryer on the main floor. But they really had no good place for them. Carrying the clothes himself was the simplest solution. He picked up the walker now and carried it behind his mom. She seemed very stable that day so he didn't rush to keep up. He tossed the "infernal contraption" into the trunk while she took the passenger seat.

As he started the car, he glanced over to make sure she was buckled and ready before he put it in gear.

"Here's what I'm thinking," she said.

"Yeah?"

"You should invite Ella to our house for dinner next Sunday."

Sebastian laughed. It wasn't funny that she was back on Ella. He just never expected to find himself wishing she was still talking about laundry. "What makes you think that's a good idea?"

His mom ignored the sarcasm. "If she's having to keep the evening free just for the fifteen minutes it takes to set up the gym, making her dinner first would make it more worth her while. You'd be doing her a favor, or could at least sell it that way when you ask her."

"I'm not going to invite her over to be interrogated by you."

"You know it's a good idea."

He shook his head.

"I'll let it marinate," she said as she pushed on the radio for the rest of the drive.

It was a talk show he ignored. It was usually interesting, but he didn't want to get interested in something he could only listen to for five minutes. His mom turned it off as he parked. Then she said his name in a serious tone that got his attention.

"Have you told her what really happened with Kathy?" she asked.

He only shook his head and quickly got out of the car. His mom was the only one who knew, or at least the only one who believed it. The one other person he'd told was Angie. He'd met her at work not long after college. She wasn't from Andauk and didn't know the rumors. She didn't know she was supposed to fear him.

They dated nearly six months before he decided to tell her. He worried that if any of the gossip did reach her, and she hadn't heard it from him first, then she wouldn't know what to believe. And keeping it from her made him feel he would deserve those doubts. He told her what happened the day he broke up with Kathy and some of the different versions he'd heard. He left out the stories that had surfaced since. People tried to keep those behind his back so he couldn't tell her everything anyway.

It had seemed as though she believed him, even sympathized. But the very next time they went out, he could tell something was different. He sensed her uncertainty, her growing fear. She ended the relationship not long after – quickly and in public.

Sebastian hadn't dated anyone since. He hadn't found anyone worth the risk. He could handle a little rudeness around town, a few whispers or eyes that turned away in disgust. But to have someone he loved look at him as though she was frightened Mr. Hyde would appear any moment, that was something he never wanted to experience again.

He looked around as he escorted his mom inside. He didn't see Ella or Ruth before they entered the gym.

"Are you back to doing this yourself?" His mom glanced around the room while she asked. She looked as though she was disappointed it wasn't a surprise party.

"We're early, Mom. I'm sure they'll be here any minute."

She nodded and released his arm.

"Can I trust you to stand right here while I get you a chair?" he asked.

She said nothing. Her expression suggested it was a stupid question, and probably not because she intended to stay put.

Sebastian sighed and left her anyway. It was mostly when she first stood that she wobbled, and he could fetch her a chair pretty quickly. He grabbed the entire rack, which was on wheels, and pulled it out of the closet. He was about halfway back to his mom when Ella walked in. She said hello to his mom, who walked forward a few unnecessary but stable steps to greet her.

"Is the other girl, Ruth, is she not coming?"

Ella shook her head. She glanced at Sebastian to include him. "I told her we could do without her. I see her all the time because we work together, but she mostly only sees Gabriel on weekends. I didn't want to interrupt now that I know it only takes a few minutes."

The speech sounded rehearsed, but she probably expected to be asked about Ruth. "Did you think Mrs. Donnelly was lying when she told you it would take a few minutes?" Sebastian asked. He parked the chairs and pulled one down for his mom.

"No." Ella looked momentarily uncertain, then said, "Just selling optimism."

His mom's laugh echoed through the empty gym.

Sebastian also chuckled at the generous observation as he unfolded the chair and held out an arm.

"Should I get a table?" Ella asked.

"Can you carry one by yourself?"

Ella stared at him for a moment as though she might be thinking of a witty comeback. Instead she said, "Yes," and walked away.

Sebastian's mom kept hold of his arm after she was seated just long enough to pull him forward and whisper, "I like her. You better start working on your plan."

He rolled his eyes as she let go. Then he followed Ella to get a second table. He could see only a bit of strain on her face as she carried it. No more than he saw when his mom began to grill her while she unfolded its legs.

"Did you grow up here in Andauk?"

"Yes," Ella said.

"And you've been a member of St. Jude's as long?"

"Uh... yeah."

"Are you a faith-filled person or one of those who just goes through the motions?"

Ella dropped the table on its side. She'd only gotten it an inch or two off the ground, but the noise still radiated her surprise.

"Mom, I don't think that's appropriate." Sebastian had caught up just in time.

"Why not?" she asked. "We're at a church. That's an appropriate place to ask a question about faith."

He tried not to sound as though he was scolding a child. "But you ask it as though there's a right answer."

"There is a right answer," she said. "I was once a going through the motions person, and I know what's better."

He looked at Ella with a quick head shake to tell her she didn't have to say anything.

But she turned to his mom, despite her clear embarrassment, and said, "I'm not going through the motions. Most of the time."

The answer earned her a laugh. His mom said through her chuckle, "That's exactly right. You don't ever want to get complacent and feel as though you're faith-filled *enough*. Isn't that what I've told you?"

Sebastian nodded because he'd definitely heard that before.

Ella appeared pleased to have passed the test but not eager for another. She started pulling down chairs and unfolding them with enough noise to drown out questions. His mom still got in a few, simple things about her family and her job. Then Mrs. Johnson showed up early to chat and took some of the pressure off. With company, Sebastian didn't mind leaving his mom as soon as everything was in place. The last thing he set up was her walker. She smiled and waved as he left, carefully keeping her eyes from going anywhere near the walker.

Ella went through the doors ahead of him. He expected she was already on her way home. She actually waited for him though, was stopped just outside and facing his way. "That was at least as fast as last week," she said.

"I can still start timing us if you like."

She shook her head. "Just an observation, not a challenge."

"Did you walk here?" He didn't see her car in the parking lot.

"Yeah."

"It's a nice day for a walk."

"Yeah, I thought so." She hesitated, then said, "Are you going home to stare at the wall?"

"It's still more fun than bingo."

She laughed lightly but still seemed nervous. "It's so nice I thought I'd take a long way home."

Sebastian couldn't help thinking that sounded like an invitation. Was it an invitation or just wishful thinking on his part? Was it a sign of the beginning of trust? He held his questions as a fairly old man was heading their way for bingo. Sebastian waited until he was close before he opened the door for the man, who was plodding along with a cane. When he slowed, Sebastian thought the old man might be having trouble navigating the turn into the building before he realized he intended to stop. The man looked between Sebastian and Ella with a frown.

Ella took a step backwards, presumably concerned that they were in his way.

There was a rough sound of throat clearing before the man said, "Perhaps you should leave this young woman alone."

The suggestion was so surprising that Sebastian didn't know what to say to it. Had he missed some cue that Ella was trying to get away? She had shrunk back farther with one hand needlessly straightening her glasses, but the fidgeting seemed to be in response to the interruption.

The old man was focused only on Sebastian. He took advantage of Ella's movement to place himself between them. "You the one who's hard of hearing?" he growled.

Ella turned around and walked quickly away from the scene, which left Sebastian with no reason to stay. He pulled the door he was holding even wider. "I'm on my way home."

The man wobbled through the door without looking back. Sebastian held his position a bit longer as two more bingo players were approaching. He recognized one from his mom's card club. She smiled and thanked him as she entered, her friend on her heels.

Ella had already disappeared by the time he started walking to his car. He tried to see the humor in being confronted by a frail old man. With his stooped posture, he was a foot shorter. Sebastian could have knocked him over without even touching him, just kick the cane he'd been leaning on. Ineffective or not, the misguided protection would still have been admirable if it hadn't scared Ella away. That was the part that kept him from laughing.

7

Ruth looked into the burrito where she'd just taken a bite. "Mmm," she said thoughtfully. "It's not bad."

Ella peeled back the tin foil on hers. It smelled delicious, but it smelled like pizza sauce. The incongruity of sight and smell was making her nervous. The local pizza place had added what they called a pizza burrito to their menu a few months earlier. Ella and Ruth had been trying to prod each other into trying one. It occurred to Ella that the pizza burritos might be removed from the menu if no one ordered them and then they'd miss their chance to try the experiment. She and Ruth both got one for their Friday lunch treat.

"Try it," Ruth said. She took another bite.

They did need to get back to work eventually. Ella decided to be bold and took a mouthful rather than a nibble. Wonderful flavor hit her tongue the same time a blob of sauce hit her chin. She grabbed her napkin. "This is good," she said, "but I'm not sure it's the best thing to eat outside. I'm going to be lucky not to get any of this on my lap." It was basically pizza toppings wrapped in a tortilla rather than slapped on a crust.

"We have to," Ruth said. "It's been so rainy this week, we've hardly had a chance to talk."

Ella nodded. "I'm glad it's warmed up again. It'll feel more like an ice cream night tonight."

"Tonight's the night," Ruth said with a grin.

"I know. It's the night it won't work."

"Yes, it will." Ruth unfolded the tin foil enough to set her lunch in her lap while she attacked her fingers with a napkin. "We have lots of ideas. I can ask Joseph about the new art for June. I can ask Heather if she finished the book she borrowed. I can also say it's a good time to check with Eric about the anniversary dinner he and Gabriel are planning for their parents. One of those people will have chairs I can move to. And if everything is full, I can always have a sudden desire to hold my niece. I can do that standing behind Isaac and Jessica."

"What about Gabriel?" Ella asked. "Is he going to stand around while you hold Grace?"

"Yeah. He knows the plan."

"He does? How much did you tell him?"

Ruth sent a reassuring smile. "Not everything. I just told him I was doing some matchmaking so he should follow me if I leave the table at some point. He tried to tell me not to interfere, but he'll still come with me."

"It's not going to work," Ella said.

"Yes, it is. And I tried to get some information from Isaac, too."

"About Sebastian?"

"Yeah. I talked to Isaac last night. You know he's always insisted Sebastian is a good guy but never elaborates. And I do respect that he wants to stay out of any gossip." Ruth took a quick bite while Ella waited for someone to elaborate. "Anyway, I asked if his opinion would be any different if I started dating Sebastian." She waved the napkin around as she talked. "He tried to give me a hard time about shouldn't I be more concerned about what Gabe would think, and I told him I was serious. So he got serious. He said, 'I honestly believe Ella would be in no danger.'"

Ella cringed. "He knew you were asking for me?"

"Yeah," Ruth said, "but I've been talking about trying to fix you up with someone for a long time so he probably thinks I came up with it on my own."

That was only a little better, but Ella did trust Isaac's opinion.

"Then he said that at work, where no one knows his reputation, there are a couple of guys who call him Squeaky."

"Squeaky?" Ella assumed this was not a flattering nickname, but she didn't understand it.

"As in, squeaky clean," Ruth said. "Apparently they invited him to go out drinking with them to try to pick up women and Sebastian told them he doesn't drink and that a bar was the last place he'd want to meet a woman. Then they started calling him Squeaky behind his back."

"Wow, he can't win, can he?" Ella observed. "He's shunned for being bad at home and mocked for being good at work."

"It's just those two guys, and Isaac said most people don't pay them any attention. It sounds as though he's mostly respected at work. It was, after all, Sebastian's recommendation that got Isaac hired."

"True." Ella nodded. "I suppose I can put that in a list of reasons that *maybe* I *might* be allowed to hope."

Ruth snorted. "Like you need more reasons."

Ella threw a jab into Ruth's side with her elbow. But then she sighed. "The plan still isn't going to work because the first step is for Sebastian to come and sit by me, and he's not going to want to after what happened on Sunday.

"The old guy?" Ruth waved her hand dismissively. "He's not going to be there so you have nothing to worry about."

"I still think Sebastian is mad at me for not... I should have said he wasn't bothering me."

Ruth shook her head longer than necessary because she kept shaking it until she finished chewing. "No. We already talked about this. That guy told Sebastian to get lost because of what he thought he knew about him, not because of anything he actually saw. Nothing you said would have changed that."

"It still would have been the right thing to do." Ella took another bite. Unfortunately, her pizza burrito was becoming less enjoyable, not because of diminishing flavor but because of her guilt.

"You were scared," Ruth said.

"Because I'm a coward."

"You simply missed an opportunity." Ruth wiped more of the messy lunch from her face before she looked at Ella apologetically. "I hate to say it, but I have a feeling if you start to see more of Sebastian you may see more... opportunities."

Ella chuckled at the phrasing but groaned at the same time. Ruth was right. There had been looks and comments already that proved it. If Ella chose to spend time with Sebastian, she'd likely be pressed to defend that choice.

"Hey, do you think your dad knows?"

"Uh..." Ella didn't know if they were still talking about the same thing. The question was sudden. "About what?"

"That we come out here to talk about things we don't want him to hear?"

"Probably," Ella said with a laugh. "But I suspect he appreciates it. Whenever my mom gets started about if any new guys came on a Friday or some guy she wants to fix me up with, he immediately thinks of something that needs to be done in a different room."

Ruth smiled and wadded up her now empty foil.

"Anything new with you?" Ella asked. "A wedding date perhaps?" Ruth would have told her, but she still wanted to show some interest.

"No. Honestly, I think I've been doing a bit better at not thinking about it. Just trying to be happy with where we are." She paused. Smiled. "I mean, I'm lucky, right? A lot of people my age haven't even found the person they want to marry."

Ella definitely couldn't argue with that. She was two years older than Ruth and still floundering. There was a bit of hope when she thought of Sebastian, but she didn't want to think of him any more just then. She was nervous enough about the big plan. "Well," she said, "now we know what a pizza burrito tastes like."

Ruth stood from the bench and looked at the front of her outfit. "And I think we managed to do it without wearing any."

There were no red spots on Ella's clothes either. That was a tiny victory she could celebrate as they headed back into the insurance office.

The phone rang before Ella was seated at her desk. Ruth picked it up and greeted the caller. After a moment she said, "One moment, please," and put the call on hold. She looked wary as she told Ella it was for her.

Ella put the phone to her ear. She gave herself a count of three to slip into professional mode before she picked up the line. "Sweet Insurance," she said. "This is Ella. How may I help you?"

"Hi, sweetie," came a voice that Ella recognized as her mom.

She gave Ruth a dirty look for teasing her as she relaxed. "Hi, Mom. What's up?"

"I need to talk to you."

"Okay," Ella said. She had assumed that was why she called.

"At home."

"I'm at work."

"So am I," her mom said. "I mean, tonight."

"Uh… did you call me just to tell me you want to talk to me later?"

"No, I want to talk to your dad. I just wanted to say hello to you first."

"Well, hello to you, too. Should I transfer you to Dad now?"

"Yes, please. But we'll talk tonight?"

"Sure," Ella said, feeling her forehead wrinkle in confusion. She lived with her parents. There was no need to make an appointment to talk. "I'll see you tonight." She pushed the hold button, then the intercom because it was more fun than yelling into the next room. "Mr. Sweet, Mrs. Sweet is on line one for you."

Ella hung up the phone and looked at Ruth. "That was weird."

"She has something particular to talk about?"

"I guess." Ella shrugged. "She probably found out one of her coworkers has a son or a brother who's single."

The door to her dad's inner office clicked closed. He could be talking to her mom about any number of things, but Ella had an unsettled feeling that it had something to do with her and the talk her mom wanted to have later.

She put the weird call out of her mind for the afternoon of work. But dinner was weird, too. Ella helped her mom in the kitchen. The older woman kept looking as though she was about to say something, then making a comment on the weather or the food or some other bland subject that didn't seem consistent with the buildup in her expression.

Ella kind of wanted to ask what was going on. She refrained. She wasn't all that eager to dive blindly into a subject that had buildup.

The weirdness continued as they sat down to eat. After they said a prayer and began to tuck into the meal, it was too quiet. It wasn't the natural quiet of three hungry introverts. Ella could sense her parents sending meaningful glances at each other and at her. Eventually, she decided that she'd had enough.

She set down her fork. "Okay, which of you wants to tell me what you want to tell me?"

They smiled the exact same smile at the exact moment. They looked like two people trying to appear as though they knew absolutely nothing while holding a sign that said everything they knew. Ella just couldn't read the sign.

"Seriously," she said. "You guys are starting to freak me out. What's going on?"

Her dad nodded at her mom in a clear signal to be the one to begin. Ella followed the nod to fix her attention on the dark-haired woman next to her. Ella's mom had lighter brown hair before she started going gray. Now she dyed it a darker shade than Ella's.

"Well, sweetie, we are concerned because we have heard some disturbing… no, concerning… or just possibly concerning… Are you dating Sebastian Jones?"

Ella sighed and kicked herself. She should have guessed that. "No," she said simply.

"Because someone at work said you were talking to him outside the church Sunday evening."

"Yeah, I was." Ella looked between her parents with a mixture of disbelief and annoyance. "I told you I was going over there to help him set up for bingo. It should not have been surprising, or *concerning*, to find out I talked to him while I was there."

Her mom nodded slowly. "Yes, but… I was told you were talking."

The strange emphasis did not give the word a different meaning. Ella narrowed her eyes at her mom.

"She said it looked like you were talking as though there was something between you."

Ella rolled her eyes. The only thing between her and Sebastian had been an old guy with a cane. Apparently, her mom's source missed that part. "We're not dating," she said.

She saw her dad nod out of the corner of her eye and resume eating.

Her mom, on the other hand, sort of smiled and winced and cocked her head uncertainly. She said, "I don't know whether to be happy or disappointed."

"What?"

"While I'm glad you're not seeing someone behind our backs, you know I'd still like for you to be seeing someone."

"Just not Sebastian?" Ella asked.

"That's not what I said." Her mom glanced across the table for support.

Ella's dad smiled around a mouthful of food. He chewed slowly.

"Yes, the man has a certain reputation. But we all know some of the stories are ridiculous." Her mom adopted a skeptical tone. "How many times are we supposed to believe he's gotten arrested without spending time in jail? Besides, you're a smart girl. We know you're a pretty good judge of character."

"Then why were you and Dad sitting here all shifty-eyed like you were so concerned you had to stage an intervention?"

Her mom smiled at being called shifty-eyed.

Ella's dad finally waded into the conversation as he said, "Because we were afraid you were hiding it from us."

"Exactly. Keeping a relationship secret is a much bigger

warning sign than any third-hand rumors."

That did make sense. Ella forgave her parents for the odd behavior because of the legitimate worry behind it. She had been tempted to hide relationships in the past just to keep her mom from getting excited, but that felt wrong.

She ate some of her dinner while it was still warm. Or at least not cold. She was distracted though, still thinking about how easily her parents seemed to dismiss Sebastian's dangerous reputation. Would they have done that if she hadn't just said she wasn't dating him? They were chatting about her brother. He was still in school and taking a summer class. They were talking about what they remembered from calculus. The comments were not interesting enough to keep her curiosity about some what-ifs in check.

During a lull when her dad was trying to recall some mathematical term, Ella casually asked, "What would you guys think if I *was* dating him?"

Her dad's eyes dropped to his plate where he was chasing a rolling pea with his fork and trying to appear as though the quest needed his full focus.

Her mom said, "What do you mean?" Then held her breath.

"I mean, would you… would you still overlook the things you've heard if I…"

Ella's mom had eyes the same shade of brown as her own, but they seemed darker in contrast to the whites she exposed. "Are you saying…!?"

"I'm not saying anything. I'm just… hypothetically," Ella said.

"So you are interested in him?"

"Mom, I'm only asking what if."

"What if?" she said. "If the guy is my ticket to grandmahood, then I don't care what anyone else says."

Ella did some controlled stabbing of her plate to show her frustration. "I didn't say he was or even could be anyone's ticket to anything."

There was a light chuckle from her dad's side of the table. "Don't forget about mother-in-law-hood."

Her mom scoffed. "I will make an excellent mother-in-law."

"Guys!" Ella glared at both of them. "You are getting so far ahead of… It's not funny."

"Ahead?" Her mom sucked in an excited breath. "We're not wrong, just ahead?"

There was no way around this, only through it. "Fine," Ella said. "There may be a possibility that I would consider dating him *if* he asked me."

"Thank you, now we can be serious." Her mom's tone lost the teasing and traces of insanity. "We would treat Sebastian like any other guy in your life. There would be some level of interrogation and testing to make our own judgments on whether or not he's a good fit for you. Ultimately though, if you trusted him, that would go a long way."

"Interrogation? Really, Mom?"

"We would want to get to know someone who might become part of the family."

"You interrogate someone who is accused of a crime, not someone you're trying to make friends with."

"Not necessarily." Her mom tipped her head thoughtfully, as though it was a philosophical conversation. "An interrogative is a statement in the form of a question. A list of questions is an interrogation. It doesn't have to have the negative connotation you ascribe."

"But it does," Ella said. She could play this game, too. "The connotation of a word comes from its regular use. People use it about talking to a bad guy. It is not appropriate in this case."

"Interview sounds so formal."

It did. Ella thought formal was better than accusatory, but she wasn't interested in debating further. "Can't you just call it a conversation? And at this point a purely hypothetical conversation?"

Her mom shook her head. "That doesn't imply lots of questions. If you bring someone – anyone – home, I will have lots of questions."

Ella went back to eating. She was not going to give her mom the satisfaction of asking her to share these questions because she looked entirely too happy to have them.

Unfortunately, she didn't need to be asked. "I'd start with easy questions about his job and any hobbies. I would also need to know how long he'd want to wait before having grandchildren."

"I assume he's going to be waiting a very long time for grandchildren."

"I mean *my* grandchildren."

Ella knew what she'd meant. She wasn't sure why she'd taken the bait.

"The bottom line is this." The deeper voice of Ella's dad was also very firm. "We'd give Sebastian a fair chance if you wanted us to, but if he ever did hurt you… no one gets away with that."

8

Ella couldn't believe it worked. And she couldn't believe she was wearing a dress. The plan to get her and Sebastian at a table by themselves at the Ice Cream Shack had worked beautifully. She and Ruth got there a few minutes early to be at the front of the line without elbowing anyone. They claimed a table in the corner. Gabriel quickly joined them. And then Sebastian sat next to Ella. At first, it had appeared that the next step would be tricky.

They had a great turnout with exactly twelve other people who exactly filled three other tables. All the excuses they'd brainstormed during the week involved filling in two seats at another table, except for the one about holding Grace. Isaac and Jessica unwittingly foiled that backup by leaving the baby with her grandmother. There were no openings. Ella doubted Ruth could come up with a plausible excuse for her and Gabriel to move. Then in a stroke of luck, Ruth's other brother Adam straggled in late. She grabbed Gabriel to keep Adam from sitting alone, something she would have done even if it wasn't part of the plan. Talk about plausible.

As for the dress, Ella had nothing against wearing a dress in general. She wore one to church at least half the time and occasionally to work as well. But she hadn't worn one that day. She had changed after work, after *not* spilling any sauce on her clothes, into a solid navy dress with lace along the hem. She thought it went well with her favorite glasses. They were neutral in front with multicolored flecks along the sides. She braided the front of her hair to hold it back. She did everything she could think of to make herself look pretty to try to get Sebastian to want to sit by her so she could talk to him about something he wasn't going to want to talk about. She dressed up for an ambush.

It was ridiculous. It was especially ridiculous considering she didn't think she'd have the guts to go through with it. They had already exchanged a bit of small talk before Ruth and Gabriel changed seats. She could usually start to relax after a few minutes with him, but she was as tense as ever because she kept thinking that she wore a dress to an ambush. Who did that?

"Is your brother coming home for the summer?" Sebastian asked.

"No."

"Where is he in school again?"

"Uh, West Virginia." Ella said it like she had to think about it because the nerves were getting in the way. Deep breath, she told herself.

Sebastian ran his spoon around the edge of his dish of ice cream without scooping up a bite. "I take it you guys aren't real close."

"No. Well..." More deep breaths. "I don't *dislike* him. But he's six years younger than I am, and we've just never really had a lot in common."

He nodded understandingly.

"I, uh..." Ella wasn't quite sure what she wanted to say. She knew Sebastian had two brothers he didn't know at all, and she wondered if she was being insensitive for sounding indifferent to a brother she could know better. "Ruth was happy to see Adam show up," she said.

"She seemed surprised to see him."

"Yeah. He hasn't had any interest in joining this group and has been basically estranged from her family since November," Ella explained. "Ruth texted him about the change for this week on a whim. She didn't think there was any chance he'd actually show up since he didn't reply to her text."

"Hmm." Sebastian still didn't seem to have much appetite for the treat in front of him. He just kept gently stabbing it. "Maybe it's a first step," he said.

Ella clammed up again because now she was talking about someone else's brother. She made a six-month estrangement seem like a big deal. Not that it wasn't a deal, but by comparison she was still being insensitive. "Have you ever met your brothers?" she asked, because apparently if she was going to be insensitive, she might as well go all out.

"No," he said with a shrug. "I don't think I'm missing anything. There's an even bigger age difference. They're nine and eleven years older than me and grew up in a different area. I suppose I should want to meet them because we have a blood connection, but... honestly, anyone who shuns my mom isn't real high on the list of people I want to know."

Ella had gotten a scoop of cookies and cream with nuts sprinkled on top. She realized she was absently using her spoon to make the nuts into a line around the edge of the bowl. She glanced up at Sebastian, who had gone quiet.

He seemed amused by something. "Are there any other brothers we should talk about?"

"Oh, I shouldn't have said anything about Adam." Was she guilty of gossiping? Was she guilty of gossiping in front of a guy who had every right to hate anyone who would do that?

"Why not?" His eyes wrinkled as they looked towards Adam and back.

"Because... I didn't mean to..." He seemed confused enough that maybe he hadn't meant they were talking about brothers in a bad way. "Is it always gossip if you talk about someone who isn't present?" she asked. "I only wanted to explain why Ruth was surprised."

"I know."

"Okay." Ella regretted saying anything when Sebastian clearly wasn't thinking she might be an evil gossipmonger. Only she thought that because gossip and rumors and lies were dominating the space in her head. She needed to ask and get it over with if she ever wanted to have a normal conversation.

She scanned the room for her protection. Isaac was closer. He had his back to her and Sebastian but was easily within shouting distance. Joseph was only a little farther and was facing Ella. She could simply wave a hand to flag him down. But even as she looked for Ruth's bothers, she was sure she wouldn't need them. Sitting there with Sebastian, as nervous as she was, she still could not imagine him saying or doing anything that would make her feel threatened.

His spoon swirled the ice cream to a point. The impression he was giving at the moment was of someone deliberately eating slowly as an excuse to keep sitting there. Of course, she might have only been projecting what she was doing.

Sebastian's head stayed tilted towards his dish while his eyes lifted slowly. It was one of those looks that made her chest fill with warmth. It occurred to Ella in that moment that she might only trust him because she wanted to trust him. And if she really trusted him, she'd give him a chance to tell his side. "What happened to Kathy?" she blurted.

Unfortunately, she had blurted timidly. It came out mumbled and incoherent enough that Sebastian said, "I'm sorry. I didn't hear you."

Now or never, she told herself. She had his full attention and could clearly see any reaction. "I was trying... I was wondering if you'd tell me what really happened... with Kathy."

There was a flicker of surprise, but no anger. Ella wasn't sure what she read in his eyes. It might have been guilt or only resignation. His eyes dropped to study the ice cream. Maybe she only saw a reluctance to address an old topic. It sort of looked like fear. It definitely wasn't anger, and that was the most important answer.

"I'm sorry," she said quickly. "I shouldn't ask. People probably ask all the... I'm sorry."

"Don't apologize." He took a deep breath and put down his spoon. "I want you to know. I just don't want to have to tell you."

"Oh." Her knees started shaking under the table. How uncomfortable was this conversation going to be?

"This doesn't paint me in a very good light, but I hope you'll remember I was a lot younger."

She nodded. She'd done some stupid things as a teenager, too. Stupid was forgivable.

"The really awful part is that I never liked Kathy to begin with," Sebastian said. "We were both seniors. I asked her out on a whim, just had a thought she'd say yes and..." He shrugged.

Ella tried to look as though she was listening attentively but not too eagerly.

"We just saw a movie and then the next day at school I found out she had already told people we were a couple. I went along with it because... well, I guess I liked the *idea* of having a girlfriend. Social validation and all that. I... hung out with her when I could, usually at her suggestion. The more I knew her, the more I didn't like. She said horrible things behind her friends' backs and laughed at me and… But I was a coward. I thought if I broke up with her, she'd either cry or get angry. I didn't want to deal with that. We ended up staying together the rest of the school year and all summer, though we didn't see that much of each other. I waited until the day I left for college to end it. I told her I was going to stop by on my way out of town.

"I knew she'd figured out my plan because as soon as I walked in the door, she said, 'I know why you're here.'" Sebastian seemed to focus more on the moment as he broke from telling the story. "I wanted to tell you about what led up to that day because… I want to be completely honest so you'll believe me. I never meant to hurt her, but it was a terrible relationship from the start, and I played a part in that."

He seemed to expect a response so Ella said, "Okay," and nodded for him to keep going.

"She was angry and tried to talk me out of it," Sebastian said. "I didn't understand the anger because I didn't think she liked me all that much either. But we were both yelling. She said that if I broke up with her, she was going to tell everyone that she dumped me. I said…" He winced with remorse. "I said I didn't care what she told people as long as I never had to see her ugly face again. The rest happened so fast. She picked up… There was a statue of some kind on a shelf next to her. She picked it up and pulled her arm back. I didn't know if she intended to hit me with it or smash it or… But I reached out and grabbed her arm to stop her and somehow knocked her off balance. She fell, and she was still holding the statue and got hit in the face with it. I couldn't see how bad it was because she had her hand over her face, but there was blood between her fingers."

Ella gasped, which was when she realized how caught up she was in the story. It didn't feel like something that happened years ago. It felt like Sebastian was reliving it for her benefit. She felt awful for asking the question that put him through that.

He continued as though he hadn't heard the gasp. "I was about to run to the kitchen for a towel or ice… maybe both. I didn't really have a plan before her dad walked into the room and demanded to know what was going on. Kathy started yelling that I hit her. Her dad came after me, and I ran. I beat him to my car and locked the door, but he was yelling and banging on the window. I was afraid to back up with him so close, afraid I might run over his foot. But I was more afraid he was going to break the window, drag me out, and beat me to a pulp. I have not seen a rage like that before or since. I just drove slowly, praying he'd get his foot out of the way in time. I half expected him to get his car and follow me, but I guess he decided to stay and tend to Kathy. When he didn't show up at school the rest of the day, I figured it was over. Finally, it was over."

Ella shook her head sadly at the relief. This whole time, he'd been telling her how the gossip had started. She knew nothing was over.

"My mom called me a few days later," Sebastian said. "She told me that Kathy was walking around town with stitches and a large bruise around her eye and her arm in a sling. The story was that I beat her up when she tried to break up with me. My mom asked me what really happened. She believed me, and that was all that mattered at the time. I didn't come home again until Christmas. My mom and I went to a basketball game at the high school. There were whispers. Some people stared; others quickly averted their eyes. I could feel the attention I drew. It was like a living thing that followed me around the gym. My mom, who as you know has faced her share of public disapproval, assured me it would blow over in time." He paused to smile, a full joking smile. "She never tried to guess how much time."

"How can you make light of it?" Ella asked. "Doesn't it make you angry?"

"That's exactly how." His expression said he was trying to be confusing on purpose.

It teased a smile out of her. "What do you mean?"

"This is one of those things where people say you have to either laugh or cry. I have to look for the humor or... Anger won't do any good. Besides, who would I be angry at?"

"Kathy."

He nodded at her quick answer. "I was for a while. But I can't fault her for blaming me in the heat of the moment because I did feel responsible."

"You didn't hit her," Ella insisted.

"I did knock her down though. It was my fault she got hurt whether it was an accident or not. And after her dad's reaction I can see how it would be really really hard for her to change her story."

"I still don't know how she could just go around lying."

"I'm sure it wasn't all her," Sebastian said. "Her dad probably told people how he found me standing over her. I'm guessing a few neighbors heard or saw him yelling at me about hurting her. I ran, which made me look guilty. Lots of people knew we were dating but not entirely getting along. Plus, there was evidence on her face that *something* happened, and I wasn't around to tell my side."

"Kathy doesn't... she hasn't lived around here for some time, has she?" Ella asked. "I'm not sure I remember her."

"Were you... were you in high school the same time I was?"

He appeared to be thinking, possibly doing some math.

"Yes. I was a freshman when you were a senior."

"Hmm. Do you remember me from then?"

"Only vaguely," she said. It was a small enough town that she'd heard his name, but it wasn't until he became rather infamous that she really knew who he was.

"You're saying I was not memorable?" He frowned as though she'd just insulted him.

Ella knew he was kidding. They had no classes together and very little reason to have crossed paths. She still started to feel guilty for maybe not paying enough attention until she had a comeback. "Uh, you just asked *if* I was there, which means you don't remember me at all."

He opened his mouth for a second before he said, "You asked if Kathy still lived in Andauk. Her whole family moved away at some point while I was in college. So I can't blame them for anything that's been said since."

"They still pushed it," Ella said.

"Pushed what?"

"The snowball."

"I suppose." He shrugged. "But it always comes back to the fact that being angry solves nothing. In this case, it would even make things worse because if I got angry in public, it would only add fuel to... I once heard a quote and I don't remember the source but it's that holding a grudge is like drinking poison and expecting someone else to die." He put on a cheesy smile. "I'm not drinking the poison."

Ella smiled at the idea that he simply chose happiness. Where had she heard that before? "I guess it would be hard to... Can you imagine if you tried to keep a list?"

"What kind of list?"

"You know…" She mimed writing an imaginary list on her hand. "So-and-so told three people about a girl from Sandusky so I'll be mad at her for three years and so-and-so only told one person but said Kathy was in a coma so…"

Sebastian had started laughing. "Yeah, I wouldn't have time to be angry if I was trying to keep records."

"And where would you find reliable sources for unreliable information?" Ella asked. She couldn't believe the conversation she'd been stressing over for two weeks was actually making her laugh.

"For appropriate length of grudge, I'd probably have to know motivation, too."

"Motivation?"

"Intent counts," he said. "You know some people just like a good story, the juicier the better. But others… If you honestly believed a guy was dangerous, wouldn't you feel obligated to warn someone you thought might get mixed up with him?"

That question wasn't funny. A year ago, Ella had fully believed that Sebastian was dangerous. She'd thought that even when she knew half of what she heard about him was exaggerated. She'd never bothered to consider how much, if any, was true. If she hadn't spent the last eight or nine months starting to know him personally, she'd be one of the people giving out "helpful" warnings.

"Goodness! You guys are the slowest eaters ever." Ruth was suddenly standing at the edge of their table.

Ella looked down and saw that she had half a bowl of ice cream soup she'd completely forgotten about.

"Adam already left," Ruth said. "Joseph wants to lead the rest of us in a prayer circle before we start breaking up. He thinks we need to remember we're a church group even when we're having fun. God in all things or something. Come on." She waved a hand for them to follow where the others were already forming a circle.

Ella felt herself reddening to see everyone waiting for her. And then she took her place in a seriously lopsided circle. The group held hands in a line that snaked between tables to form an unusual shape. That wasn't the only reason it felt lopsided. She held Ruth's hand on one side, which was fine. Sebastian held her other hand, which caused heat and trembles and obsession over whether she was squeezing too tightly or hanging on like a limp rag.

Sebastian asked if she was going to finish her ice cream when the group was done. When she shook her head, he offered to clear the table. The others began to say goodbyes and split up. Ella ended up out the door with Ruth without saying anything else to Sebastian, though he'd waved.

Ruth hurried them towards her car as she asked, "How'd it go?"

"Pretty good, I think."

"I saw you guys laughing some, and that seemed like a good sign. Unless you didn't get a chance to ask."

Ella nodded.

"You did ask him?"

"I did."

"And?" Ruth's red eyebrows shot up expectantly.

"He... It sounded like an accident."

"And you believe him?" Ruth asked. "It's important that you really think he was sincere and aren't just letting all the mushiness get in the way."

Ella nodded again. "I really believe him."

"I'm impressed."

"Why?"

Ruth chuckled. "You looked a little green when I left you alone. I wasn't sure you could go through with it."

"Neither was I," Ella admitted.

"It's funny how different you can be."

"What do you mean?"

"Well..." Ruth scrunched up her nose. "At work, you can get a customer on the phone and be like, 'You have this many days. We get your payment by this date or your policy is canceled, end of story.'" She eyed Ella appraisingly. "You do have a backbone. It just disappears sometimes."

"I know." There was nothing Ella could say to refute that without lying. "It's different at work," she said. "I feel anonymous on the phone. They can't see me, and I'm just that girl from the insurance company. But face to face, especially if it's someone I don't know, I have to be me. That's... scarier."

Ruth smiled. "When you said especially someone I don't know, I thought you were going to say especially if it's someone cute."

"Well, that doesn't help either," Ella said with a laugh.

9

Sebastian was smiling to himself at how comfortable Ella had seemed after they talked. She was really starting to be herself around him. He'd barely gotten their ice cream cups into the trash when Isaac stopped him. "Hey, Sebastian," he said, "can I talk to you a second?"

"Sure. What's up?"

"I hate to be the one to tell you this, but there's a rumor."

Sebastian felt his eyes roll. "There's always a rumor."

"I think maybe you need to know about this one. And I need you to know that I don't believe it."

"Thanks," Sebastian said. "But like I said, there's always a rumor."

"This one's different. It's not some nameless girl in another town. It's... your mom."

"My mom? What about my mom?"

Isaac winced regretfully. "People are saying she's been showing up places covered in bruises."

"Bruises? You mean, bruises caused by me?"

"That's what I heard," Isaac said.

His mom? People were involving Sebastian's mom in their trashy entertainment? The thought threatened to make him angry. He plastered a smile on his face anyway. "I guess I shouldn't be surprised that she's finally fallen victim to my violent rampages."

Isaac smiled faintly at the sarcasm. "I don't suppose there's anything you can do to get ahead of it, but... well, now you know."

"Thanks."

Jessica came up to Isaac's elbow with a sympathetic expression. She smiled around it as she said hello and goodbye. Sebastian did appreciate the show of support, but it was difficult to let it penetrate while the news was so fresh.

He drove straight home. His mom was sitting in her usual chair with her usual blanket and puzzle book. The walker was nowhere in sight so she hadn't used it to get there. She looked somehow smaller and more vulnerable. Her white curls were slightly matted near the back in a place she might no longer be able to reach. There was no way she'd let him start brushing her hair for her though.

The larger bruise on her forearm had healed enough that it was yellowy and indistinct around the edges. A smaller one appeared fresh and dark higher on her arm. He hadn't worried about the bruises because she assured him they didn't hurt at all. He'd been an idiot not to realize how they would look with his reputation.

But what was he supposed to do? Ask her to keep fully covered in the summer? Tell her to act as though there was something to hide?

She looked up from her puzzle. "Something wrong?"

"Um..." He didn't want to lie. He came and sat near her. "You going to be up much later?"

"I napped longer than usual this afternoon," she said. "Why don't you tell me about your group tonight?"

He shrugged. "Not a lot to tell."

"Ella wasn't there?"

"She was." He still didn't want to lie, but that didn't mean she was getting more than basic facts.

"You just didn't get to talk to her?"

Sebastian gave her a look that he hoped said she was barking up the wrong tree for information.

"Well…" She eyed him shrewdly. "I just know my baby usually comes home with a spring in his step on Fridays. But not tonight."

There were a few things wrong with what she'd said. Sebastian didn't think he'd ever in his life had a spring in his step so she was either pretending to see something she didn't or imagining it. Also, he didn't like being referred to as her baby. It reminded him that he was in fact her baby, her youngest child and not her only child.

It didn't bother Sebastian in the least that he had two half-brothers he'd never met because he'd never met them. Except that it hurt his mom to think of them, and he wondered if she'd been thinking of them when she called him the baby.

"We finally had everyone back at card club last night," she said.

"That's good." Sebastian wasn't particularly interested in her card club, but he was very interested in a new subject.

"Gemma just got back from visiting her first great-grandbaby. She had lots of pictures, and he's a cutie."

"How old is he?" he asked.

"Almost a whole year."

"She's not the first woman in the group to have a great-grandbaby, is she?"

"Oh, no." His mom shook her head with a dry smile. "Ellen has that honor which she reminded us repeatedly. Of course, I still don't have any regular grandbabies to display."

"How did the games go?"

She sighed. "I was partnered with Evelyn for the first one."

Sebastian smiled at his mom's dramatic disappointment. He knew Evelyn was actually her favorite woman in the card club, when she was on a different team.

"I don't know if that woman suffers from not enough math or too much optimism," she said, "but she *always* overbids."

"I'm guessing that game didn't end in your favor."

"Lost the second one, too. But that one was closer."

"Sorry it wasn't a great night," Sebastian said.

"I didn't say that." A dreamy look covered her face. "Ellen brought churros. We snacked on them between games, and there were plenty to go around. Delicious."

He nodded. That did sound good.

"But I probably shouldn't tell you I had something so decadent," she said. "It's already been way too long since you brought me one of Chip's burgers."

It had been months. Sebastian had sort of hoped she'd forgotten how much she liked them.

"I know you don't like me to eat a lot of red meat, but once in a while won't kill me."

"Is this your way of complaining about my cooking, Mom?"

She made a scoffing noise. "If you're fishing for compliments, I'm not taking the bait. You know as well as I do that nobody makes burgers as good as Burger Brothers. So when are we going to have some?"

"Maybe," he said slowly as an idea came to him, "maybe if you start using the walker, I'll bring you a burger."

"Maybe," she said it slowly, mocking his tone. "Maybe you will bring your mother a burger because you love her."

"And maybe it's because I love you that I don't want you to eat something so full of fat and salt and —"

"We don't have the heathiest diet around here," she interrupted, "so I know when you're making excuses. You're really going to hold it over my head until I start using that infernal contraption, aren't you?"

"If I have to."

She frowned and sighed heavily. "What's the plan?"

"The plan?"

"For you to win over Ella."

For crying out loud, how had she gone back to Ella. "There's no plan, Mom."

"That might be your problem," she said.

"The only problem I have is a mother who is nosy."

"Now I've been watching her, subtly of course. She's interested."

Interested? Possibly. Afraid? Certainly. Sebastian could not afford to appear aggressive. He needed to earn her trust, prove he would never hurt her, before he could suggest he'd like to spend more time with her. If there was a plan, it would only be to figure out how to receive more patience.

"You just turned twenty-nine."

He turned to his mom, wary of where she was headed by bringing up his age.

"You know what comes next, don't you?"

"Yes, Mom. I know what comes after twenty-nine," he said.

"You don't have time to dilly-dally. You need a plan if you want a family to take care of."

"What makes you think I want that?" he asked, which he knew was a stupid question because his mom wouldn't treat it as rhetorical.

"You take such good care of me that I know it isn't duty.

You're a natural caretaker, and you need people to care for after I'm gone."

That was something he didn't want to think about. His mom was already seventy-three and with a lot of health problems, but he still didn't want to think she might not be around forever.

"Plus, you need a woman who can take care of your needs." She dared to wiggle her eyebrows at him.

Sebastian stood up fast. "Good night, Mom."

He went to the kitchen to retrieve the walker he'd left there at some point. He returned to the living room only long enough to leave it near her chair where she could use it if she decided to stop being stubborn.

She stopped him in the doorway. "Sebastian?"

"Yes?"

"Are you sure nothing's bothering you?"

"You mean aside from my pushy mother?"

"Yes, aside from that?"

"I'm sure, Mom. Good night."

10

Sebastian found himself looking forward to bingo more than he had in nearly three years, which was how long he'd been taking his mom to bingo. Of course, it wasn't the game but seeing Ella beforehand that had him ready to leave before it was time.

Since they talked on Friday, it felt as though he'd been waiting for the proverbial other shoe. He knew he'd have to address the story and the rumors before their relationship could move forward. The fact that she'd been the one to bring it up was promising. She wanted to know the truth and was willing to give him a chance to tell it. Maybe there was actually a chance she wanted to move forward, too.

She'd seemed to believe him, but he'd been here before. He'd held back with Angie though. He didn't admit the unflattering backstory. He hoped that would help Ella trust him where Angie hadn't. And Ella… the stakes felt much higher with her. The past didn't seem to be tempering his hopes. What did temper them, or at least disguise them, was having his mom clinging to his arm. The last thing he needed was for her to imagine some sort of spring in his step and start prying into the cause.

Just before they got to the door, Ella popped out and held it open for them.

"Ella! How nice to see you again." His mom beamed at the

young woman before she left Sebastian with the walker to go inside first.

"Hello," Ella said. Her eyes moved to him as she tacked on a smile.

Sebastian returned the greeting. "Hi." He stopped himself from relieving her of the door. She might have thought he was reaching for her. Plus, the infernal walker was in his way.

His mom sighed loudly and shook her head at him. "You're supposed to hold the door for ladies, you know."

"She... got there first," he said lamely.

"This time," Ella said. She looked back and forth between them and appeared to be thinking quickly as the door closed behind her. "If we were keeping track of who got the door more, it would definitely not come out in my favor." Her tone was light.

Sebastian's mom nodded seriously. She seemed to be gloating about something as she turned into the gym.

Ella followed. Her face was turned away, but Sebastian could tell she was smiling to herself.

"I'll grab the chairs," he said.

"I'll come with you." His mom grabbed his arm. "My legs could use a stretch."

He walked the pace of a death march. Ella came along just as slowly. She was on his other side but kept a step behind. Sebastian couldn't help thinking how nice it would be if Ella grabbed his other arm. He wouldn't care how long it took to cross the gym if she was clinging to him. He looked down at his mom with a bit of concern. Were her legs really hurting her?

She winked. "Ella," she said, "I don't suppose I could talk you into staying for a game tonight?"

"Oh, I, uh... I don't think so."

"It just seems a shame for you to come all the way over here for a few minutes of work."

"I live right around the corner," Ella said. "It's not a big deal."

"Still… it would be nice if we could think of an incentive for you." She looked up at Sebastian as though that was his cue.

He frowned at her for thinking he would jump into her plot.

Ella said, "I like helping."

His mom sighed. "Yes, but it only takes a few minutes."

"Not at this pace," Sebastian mumbled.

He thought he heard Ella squelch a laugh. She jumped ahead of them as they reached the closet but stepped back again to let Sebastian open it. She apparently learned her lesson.

He pulled the door open and his mom let go for a moment as he wheeled out the large rack of chairs. She stepped over to Ella. "Do you mind if I take your arm for a while? I'm probably an easier burden than that rack, and my son will have a heart attack if I walk without holding onto something."

Ella lifted her arm from her side to allow an easier handle.

Sebastian pushed the cart ahead of them to get things moving. He heard his mom asking Ella about her plans for the evening. She had none. Her parents were out for the night so she would be alone. He refrained from looking back as his mom would likely be looking at him as though that was another cue. Ella wisely asked some questions about bingo to get to a safer subject. Then the racket of unfolding chairs began. The room was set up quickly. Sebastian's mom was in her favorite place with at least one fellow player to keep her company, and he was heading outside on Ella's heels.

She stopped outside, looking uncertain. "That was… I guess I'll go home now."

He tried to word a suggestion that would be easy to reject, in case he was wrong about her being open to other options. "Are you looking forward to a little time alone?"

"Not particularly."

"How would you feel about some company?"

Her eyes flickered to the ground and back several times while she apparently tried to smile and tried not to smile at the same time. "I, um, I wouldn't want to take you away from the wall you like to stare at."

He enjoyed the joke almost as much as the confirmation that she would stay with him. "I have an idea," he said. "What if we go around town looking for things that are more fun than bingo?"

Ella let out a surprised laugh. "Okay. Where should we start?"

"If we know where we're going, it's not a quest."

"Oh," she said. "It's a quest?"

She actually sounded intrigued, which was awesome because Sebastian felt he might be trying too hard. "Let's go this way," he said. He knew there was a playground behind the school so he might have been cheating already. But he knew the town too well not to cheat a little.

"Okay," she said, "but I think we both know this town too well to not know where we're headed."

She practically read his mind. "You sense cheating?"

"I sense there's a playground around that corner," Ella said. "But I don't know if it'll be more fun than bingo. It's made for little kids."

When they reached the edge of the mulched area, Ella walked a few steps ahead to the monkey bars. She was able to walk under them as she moved her hands from bar to bar. She turned to

Sebastian still holding the last bar and said, "This is so much easier than I remember."

He smiled and nodded towards the swings. They all appeared to be about the same height so he just tried the one on the end. It was uncomfortably low. Ella sat next to him. Her knees were also high enough that swinging would be a challenge, though it looked like she could manage it.

Sebastian shook his head. "I don't think this is going to work."

Ella didn't seem at all disappointed as she stood up and said, "It wouldn't be much of a quest if we don't even have to leave the church."

"I suppose not," he said. "You lead, and I'll follow." He gestured for her to choose a direction.

She looked him right in the eye. "You want me to lead so I get the blame if we can't find anything more fun."

"I can't believe you doubt," he said. "This is already more fun."

"I guess you did set the bar pretty low."

He began to walk towards Main Street just to get them moving. They walked in silence for a block or two. It was actually a fairly comfortable silence.

"You know what this reminds me of?" Ella asked after a minute. She kept talking before he could answer. "I guess it doesn't remind me of it. I just happened to think of it. Remember Mr. Fetterman's 7th grade science? You had him, right?"

"7th grade? Yeah, that was Mr. Fetterman."

"Remember we had to do a big leaf project? Did you do the one where we had to collect leaves?"

"Yeah," he said. "Like twenty or thirty leaves and identify them all in a scrapbook sort of thing."

Ella nodded enthusiastically. "I think it was twenty, but it seemed like a *lot* at the time. I was having trouble finding that many that were different, and I heard someone say she found a ginkgo tree by the high school. Ginkgo leaves are distinctive, kind of fan shaped, and I wanted one of those." She shrugged sheepishly. "I already had several maples that I wasn't sure I had correctly... I thought two might actually be the same type and... I wanted one I was sure I'd get right. So I went on something like a quest."

Sebastian smiled at the word. "That's why it reminded you."

"Uh huh. I went to the high school," she said, "and I couldn't find the tree. I walked farther away, several blocks and kept coming back in circles because I was afraid I missed it. You want to guess how long it took me to find that ginkgo leaf?"

"An hour?" he said.

She shook her head.

"Two hours?"

She paused a moment before shaking her head with her lips pressed against a smile.

Sebastian thought he might have been impressed by the determination if Ella didn't look so amused by it. That was contagious. "Three hours?" he guessed.

Ella nodded and said, "Nearly. I spent nearly three hours wandering around town before I found that leaf."

"At least you found it."

She smiled. "But that's not the end of the story."

"You didn't drop it, did you?"

"Oh, no. It was secure," she said. "I was walking home, feeling triumphant, when I passed another ginkgo tree. It was in front of a house only two down from mine. And it had been there the whole time."

"I'm guessing you felt a little less triumphant," he said,

smiling at the story and how comfortable she seemed while telling it. There had been at least a small shift in the relationship.

"The worst part," Ella continued, "was that it was in the direction of the jr. high. I realized I'd been walking past that tree on my way to and from school. For the next two weeks, or however long we worked on that project, I felt like the tree was laughing at me whenever I passed it."

"How about we head that way and give it a little kick for old times' sake?"

"I think," Ella said, "that would hurt me more than it hurt the tree."

Sebastian nodded. He'd only been kidding and mentioned it because Ella had begun to kick a rock down the sidewalk. It was roughly two inches in diameter and rounded enough that it tumbled rather than slid along the concrete. She was tapping it so that it stayed no more than a foot or two in front of her.

Sebastian stuck his foot between hers and the rock to give it a tap. They took turns for a while, alternating diagonal kicks to each other. But it gradually turned competitive as they kicked harder, less towards each other, and rushed to catch up to it. Until the rock deflected off a crack in the sidewalk and bounced several feet into someone's yard. Neither of them seemed to think it worth the trouble to fetch it from the grass.

Especially Ella, who said, "I can't believe we were just playing kick the rock."

Sebastian smiled at her. "You can't believe we were playing kick the rock or you can't believe it was more fun than bingo?"

She laughed. "Oh. We found one. I guess I'm pretty good at leading quests after all."

"I thought I was leading."

She seemed to consider before she shook her head. "No, I'm taking credit for the rock," she said dryly.

"Do you smell that?" Sebastian wasn't trying to change the subject. His nose had suddenly picked up a scent he couldn't ignore, some sort of meat on a grill.

"Yes." Ella nodded as she inhaled. "I don't know what that is, but someone's having a late dinner that smells really good."

"Do you think we should start knocking on doors to find it?" he asked. "Maybe we could get invited in."

"I already ate." Ella said it as though he'd been serious. "But I have another idea."

He liked the playful tone. "Really? What is it?"

She nodded towards something ahead. "Do you see that light blue house coming up on the other side of the street?"

"Yeah."

"It looks like they have a porch swing," she said. "I bet that one wouldn't be too small for us like the ones at the school."

"You want to go sit on a random porch swing?"

An uncharacteristically mischievous smile bloomed as she nodded.

Sebastian had a hard time believing sweet, shy Ella would suggest something so bold. Until he realized that she wouldn't. "You know who lives there, don't you?"

She laughed at being caught. "Yeah. My great aunt lives there. And I know she's out of town for the weekend."

"Do you think she'd mind if we borrow her swing for a few minutes?" he asked.

"No." She angled her walk to cross the street. "I'm sure she'd be fine with it."

The steps creaked as he and Ella climbed them, all three of them. The swing was hung so that they walked up to it, then turned around to sit down. Ella sat on the side closer to the street. Her hands rested on either side of her for only a few seconds before she laced her fingers in her lap.

He didn't know if that was simply more comfortable for her or if she was warding off an attempt to hold her hand. Regardless, he was actually glad she removed the temptation. He was determined to continue pursuing her as slowly and respectfully as possible. She might be beginning to believe he wouldn't hurt her, but she'd probably heard too many scary stories to have forgotten completely. Any remotely aggressive move might trigger some lingering fear.

Sebastian knew the patience would be worth it. He remembered when Ella talked to him like the creepy guy she was trying to be nice to only because it was the right thing to do. After months of small talk, she began treating him more like a friend.

And now, after a few real conversations, she was telling stories. She had some younger cousins she used to babysit. She talked about some of the games she played with them. She said most of the time it was an easy job because the girls loved to brush and braid hair. All she had to do was sit there and let them. But she also told him about one time they made such a mess in the kitchen she was afraid she'd never be asked to babysit again.

"But when I told my aunt what happened," Ella said, "she shrugged it off like they were used to messes and even thanked me for cleaning it up as best I could."

"Even though the sink was still orange?"

"Yeah. It was white again next time I came over so she must have known some sort of trick for cleaning up tomato sauce." Ella paused, apparently thinking about the memory. Then she asked, "Do you have any cousins?"

"I guess technically I do."

"Technically?" She winced. "Should I not have asked?"

"It's okay. It's no secret that my mom was messed up for a while, and that's where I came from," Sebastian said. "She's always been embarrassingly clear about my background. The rainbow after the storm and other metaphors that would make you gag."

Ella's mouth was battling a smile. She didn't look as though she might want to gag.

"Anyway," he said, "she only had one sibling, a brother who died in Vietnam, so no cousins on her side. My dad had two brothers and a sister, but he had been estranged from all of them for years, because of the alcohol, when he met my mom. They don't live around here and she never met any of his family. He was over fifty when I was born and the youngest so it's possible his siblings have grandkids my age. It'd be weird I think to track any of them down since I had so little connection to my dad anyway."

"Do you remember him?"

Sebastian shook his head. "My mom says I met him several times. She hoped the possibility of a family would spur him into getting sober like it had for her, but... I wasn't even three when he died. I don't remember him at all."

"Do you look like him?"

He shrugged and didn't get any words out before Ella waved her hands in the air like she was erasing the question.

"Never mind," she said. "I was just thinking that you don't look much like your mom. She's fair and short and... but never mind." She mashed her lips and nodded to herself. "If I'm going to be nosy, I might as well be really nosy. I'm gonna ask something personal, and you just say no comment if... if you want."

He signaled confirmation and waited for the question.

"I've known a few people with... uh... messed up families," Ella started. "There was a girl in high school, her parents were divorced and still constantly fighting. She said she was never going to get married because it wasn't worth the inevitable breakdown, and she'd never have kids because she didn't want to subject them to it. Then I had a class with someone in college who… I never quite understood her situation. She seemed to have a lot of siblings – but they were all half-siblings or step-siblings or – and she told me that the various parents would use the kids to get back at each other and someone was always jealous of someone else and… Anyway, she was dating a guy with similar issues, and she said as soon as they finished school they were going to get married and cut themselves off from everyone and start over on their own."

Sebastian was listening, but he didn't know what she was trying to ask. She didn't face him and pushed the swing harder with her feet. "I don't understand," he said. "You said you wanted to ask me something personal, but you didn't actually ask me anything."

"Oh, um… I guess… I think it's interesting the way the family we come from influences the family we want to have," Ella said. "So I wondered what your family makes you think about… future plans." She seemed to be trying to make her question, that still wasn't exactly a question, sound like a general sociological study. But it mostly sounded like she was asking if he wanted to get married and have kids.

It was possible she was fishing for red flags on why she should avoid a relationship with him. Even if she was hoping for red flags, he liked the idea he was getting any consideration at all. He took his time in answering, working to be honest while still speaking more about the past than any plans that might include Ella. "Well… my mom was great when I was growing up. She worked to instill a strong faith and the knowledge that we can always rely on God even when we can't rely on other people. Most of the time, I thought she and God were all the family I needed. But I admit I was occasionally jealous when other kids talked about doing things with their dads. And then… I worked at Seymour's all through high school. That was right before old man Seymour retired so it was still Seymour's. He filled in part of a void I hadn't appreciated was there. It's only in hindsight that I know how important he was. He didn't just bark orders. He led by example. He gave all kinds of advice whether I wanted it or not. I remember a couple of times he gave me bad instructions just to see if I'd ask because he always said you looked less stupid if you asked than if you just went along with something that didn't make sense. He even told me… I told him when I was going out with Kathy the first time. He specifically told me not to take her to a movie because you can't talk at a movie, and I needed to take her somewhere I could get to know her." Sebastian smiled at the warning. "Of course I ignored that advice, and we both know how well that turned out for me."

Ella chuckled lightly.

"Anyway," Sebastian said. He thought of his mom saying he needed someone to take care of. He thought of his impulses to protect Ella. "I think I want to someday be what I didn't have for someone else."

He didn't realize how vulnerable the admission made him feel until Ella said, "Oh, no."

"What?" he said, fearing he'd said something wrong.

She was checking the time. "I'm sorry," she said. "I'm making you late. You made me think of your mom, and she's going to be done with bingo in just a few minutes. I can't believe how long we've been sitting here." She stood up.

Sebastian moved more slowly because there was something very nice buried in her rushed apology, and he wanted to savor it.

"My mom always stands around chatting when I'm ready to take her home anyway. I won't be late."

She was already trotting off the porch and waited for him at the sidewalk. "The church is that way and my house is that way so I guess, um, I'll see you on Friday?"

He wanted to hug her before they went their separate ways. Just a quick friendly, but maybe not entirely friendly, hug. But a vision of her recoiling as he reached out extinguished the impulse. He only nodded and said, "Bye."

11

" I wish it was Friday," Ella said. She was eating an apple and knew it was the tastiest part of her lunch. She and Ruth packed lunches from home four days a week, sometimes even competing over whose was healthier, and treated themselves from one of the local restaurants on Fridays. It was Monday and Ella was already wishing for the takeout they'd have on Friday.

Ruth nodded understandingly. She didn't understand though because she said, "Can't wait to see Sebastian?"

"I was thinking about pizza," Ella said.

Ruth gave her a very skeptical look.

"I was," Ella insisted. "The pizza burrito didn't quite cut it. I want real pizza."

"Okay." Ruth still didn't sound as though she believed her. "I just thought you wanted to eat outside today so we could talk about Sebastian."

Ella smiled sheepishly. "Well, maybe. But I was totally thinking about food when I said I wished it was Friday." She held up her half-eaten apple as proof.

"Well, how'd it go yesterday?" Ruth asked. "You went for a walk and…"

"It was mostly good."

"Mostly?" Ruth widened her eyes in a plea for details.

"It was great," Ella said, though she could hear her voice

lacked conviction. "We talked a lot and... I talked. I think it was the first time I really relaxed and was myself around him. The time flew by."

"That is good." Ruth's smile was encouraging.

"But... I'm trying not to worry yet, but I thought by addressing the elephant in the room the other day that I sort of... sort of opened the door for him to ask me out. If he wanted to." She took one more bite before she tossed the core into the trash can near their bench.

"It's a little early to give up," Ruth said.

"I know." Ella fished in her bag for a napkin. "It's just that I didn't realize I'd gotten my hopes up until he left without trying to make plans."

"Hmm." Ruth lowered the carrot she'd been about to bite into. "So you are hoping? That's a big change from wanting to be cured of the crush yesterday."

Ella sort of internally rolled her eyes because she deserved it. "I was kidding myself when I said that," she admitted. "I already knew I wanted... I'm still going to be cautious and try to go slowly. *If* I'm not the only one interested."

"Oh, so when he does ask you out, you're going to say y...e...s...def...in...ite...ly?"

Ella laughed at the snail-like enthusiasm. There was a cracker in her hand. She pulled it back as though she might throw it at Ruth, who only laughed with her. Ella sighed as she put the cracker in her mouth and tried to pretend it tasted like pizza.

****

Only a few hours later, Sebastian was rummaging through the cupboards in his kitchen trying to decide what to make for dinner.

He'd planned to stop at the store on his way home but forgot until he was already in the driveway.

He'd also asked Emily to text him the nights Luke wasn't working so he could get one of those burgers his mom wanted. Luke was off that night, but Sebastian hadn't seen the text until he was already standing in the kitchen thinking about dinner. He didn't feel like going back out.

Unfortunately, the food options were worse than he thought. He found some spaghetti noodles, which would be quick and easy. The only sauce he found was pizza sauce. He considered making pizza. There wasn't time to let a crust rise. Perhaps he could just put the pizza sauce on the spaghetti. It actually sounded good, even if it was unusual. And as long as he was being unusual, maybe he'd stir in some corn and put cheddar on top instead of mozzarella.

He set some ingredients on the counter and stepped towards the living room to ask his mom what she thought of that creation. The doorbell rang before he got there. "I'll get it," he called.

His mom hadn't put down her pencil when he walked past the living room. Expecting someone selling something, Sebastian was surprised to find a man and a woman wearing police uniforms. "Can I help you?"

"Is this the Jones' residence?" the woman asked.

"Yes."

"You're Sebastian Jones and your mother is Teresa Jones?"

"Yes."

"Do you mind if we ask your mother a few questions?"

Sebastian stepped back to let them inside. He wondered for a split second what they could possibly think his mother had done. It only took him that long to realize it wasn't what someone thought she had done, but what someone thought had been done to her.

The woman introduced herself and her partner to Sebastian's

mom. Then she asked with a not-so-subtle glance at Sebastian if they could speak to her privately. Sebastian met his mom's eyes long enough to see if that was okay with her. When she nodded, he went into his bedroom and closed the door. He began to pace frantically behind it.

Isaac was right. This was different. This wasn't idle talk. Someone had taken it seriously enough to involve the police. What if they didn't believe his mom when she told them she was fine? Could he be arrested? Could they take her away, stick her in a home somewhere to "protect" her? For once, Sebastian wanted to be angry because anger he could control. Fear was a different animal.

He picked up the little glass bunny on the dresser and imagined hurling it against the wall. It didn't help. He couldn't muster enough anger to even enjoy the picture. He set it down and focused on pacing slowly and thinking clearly.

He heard footsteps down the hall. His mom was taking the officers into the kitchen, showing them that there was plenty of food in the house. Sebastian kicked himself for not remembering they needed groceries. He thought about the noodles and pizza sauce he left on the counter with a can of corn. Would they see it as an odd but perfectly acceptable combination? Was there any way that could be seen as careless or neglectful? Maybe it was. His mom deserved better than a meal that was thrown together.

He could hear bits of what was being said, his mom showing her medications. Anyone could tell her mind was still strong. The officers would have no reason not to believe her. They would see there was no abuse. He could do better, but there was nothing criminal. They had to see that. This misunderstanding would be easily cleared up.

Still, he knew this wouldn't be the end of it. There was a

police car sitting in front of their house for all the neighbors to see. That would certainly fuel the gossip engine. What if Ella heard about it? This wasn't like those vague stories she'd dismissed. People could honestly say they'd seen bruises and police involvement. Those concrete details would be hard for her to ignore. Should he try to tell her first? Would she come to him for the truth if she heard a rumor? *When* she heard the rumor.

Sebastian didn't know how to handle this. He was afraid he'd sound guilty if he pulled out one rumor of many to make sure she didn't believe it. And if she asked him... he was afraid he'd get angry. He wouldn't be angry at her but at whoever made her doubt. Even a hint of raising his voice might scare her. How could someone put him in this position when Ella was just starting to trust him? He was freaking out. There was no way he could talk about this calmly. Not yet. How long would it take for Ella to hear about it?

The rest of the house was quiet. He had heard his mom showing the officers out some time ago. He took one more minute to calm himself before he returned to the living room to check on her. His mom was sitting in her usual chair. She wasn't working on a puzzle though. She was just staring at the floor.

When Sebastian came in, she turned to him and said, "You knew, didn't you?"

"Why the police wanted to talk to you? Yeah."

"You knew what people were accusing you of," her voice broke and tears began to fall, "and you didn't say anything?"

He grabbed a tissue and handed it to her. "Don't cry, Mom. It doesn't matter."

"Why didn't you tell me?" She sniffed as she pulled herself together.

"This is why." He gestured to the tissue. "I knew it would upset you."

"I could have explained better."

"People are gonna think what they want to think."

She sat up straighter. "From now on, I will be much more vocal about all that you do for me. I will make sure everyone knows my baby is a good man."

"Oh, don't do that," he said with a groan. "Besides being obnoxious, it'll only make people think you're trying to hide something."

"I suppose you're right." She sighed and dabbed her nose. Then she pulled in a long breath. "Here's what I will do though… I will use that infernal walker."

Sebastian wrestled with how to accept that announcement. It was absolutely not the way he wanted to win the battle, but he did want her to use it. He wanted to protest and couldn't.

"Don't look at me like that," she said. "I'm not using it because I feel like I owe you something. I'm gonna use it because… because now I understand that if I fall and break a bone, I won't be the only one who suffers. I can't stop anyone from telling lies about my son, but I don't have to make it easy for them."

Sebastian nodded. He decided to accept whatever reasoning worked. He went to the corner where the walker had been shoved and set it in front of her.

She looked at it distastefully. "You expect me to practice or something?"

"No," he said. "I'm taking you to Burger Brothers, and you'll need this to get to the car."

"That sounds good. Fetch my sweater."

He grabbed her purse and sweater, which he carried for her while she carried the walker. She didn't really use it, only carried it in front of her. He guessed she would be able to catch herself with it that way so he said nothing about it being off the ground.

Burger Brothers had a big red-striped awning to identify it, not that anyone in Andauk didn't already know where it was. Sebastian helped his mom out of the car and held the door to the restaurant open so she could continue to carry the walker. It was fairly quiet inside as far as customers. The after-school crowd had evidently gone home. The bluegrass music was still cranked up.

A curly-haired woman on lime green roller skates popped out of the kitchen. Paula was probably approaching sixty. She had a white apron tied around her waist, which though still thick seemed significantly smaller than Sebastian remembered. Perhaps the skates weren't only for fun.

She grabbed a table with both hands and used it to push herself backwards. Then she put her hands behind her to bump off another table before pushing off the wall towards Sebastian and his mom. She moved like a human pinball and did all that before Sebastian got his mom settled in the closest booth.

Paula had a smile for both of them, but especially for the older woman. "Teresa," she said, "I don't think I've seen you in here for some time."

She sent a slightly dirty look at Sebastian before she said, "My son doesn't let me eat enough junk food. No offense."

"None taken." Paula leaned a little closer. "Don't let Chip hear you call it junk though. The man's extra crispy today."

"Isn't he always?"

Paula smiled fondly with a hand over her heart. "Of course." Chip was her husband.

Sebastian extricated himself from the conversation where extra crispy was apparently a word of warning *and* a term of endearment. Sometimes women made no sense. Chip appeared behind the register as he approached the order window. The man had a thick mustache and wore a green shirt under his apron.

"Hey, how's it going?" Sebastian said.

Chip said nothing. The moustache didn't even twitch. His eyes moved deliberately to the menu posted above him and then back.

"No small talk today?" Sebastian said, though that was far from surprising.

Chip raised a hand over the buttons of his cash register.

"Two standard burgers with fries. Just water to drink. Please."

A soft guttural sound came out of Chip as he entered the order. It might have been a sigh. Then he pointed at the card reader.

Sebastian paid and stepped aside.

Paula zipped past him as she returned to the kitchen.

Two middle-aged guys Sebastian didn't know had moved up to order. The first one asked for a regular cheeseburger with no mustard.

"Standard," Chip corrected as he entered it.

The other guy had the nerve to ask for a regular burger after the first guy had been corrected. Chip just stared at him for an extra moment before he pushed the button.

But then the guy said, "Can I get that with no onions or tomatoes and actually... can you make it a cheeseburger but with Swiss cheese?"

Chip put one hand on either side of the counter and leaned forward to knock his forehead against the register.

Sebastian had to turn away to keep from laughing.

Emily had just appeared in the pickup window. She put her hand over the side of her mouth to cover it and whispered,

"Someone painting over the Mona Lisa again?"

He nodded.

"I guess you got my message," she said in her normal voice.

"Yeah, thanks," he said. "I had no idea what to make for dinner so it was a great night to go out."

"I've been there." She glanced over his shoulder to where his mom was waiting. "Next time you can bring Ella."

He didn't immediately know what to say, which apparently showed.

Emily smiled. "Oh, everyone knows," she said. "But don't worry, we're rooting for you."

"Uh, thanks," he said. But he did worry. If *everyone* knew, then he'd been more aggressive than he thought.

He remembered following Ella into Granny's Shelf and standing by while Mrs. Donnelly tricked her into helping him with bingo and the way he'd made a beeline for her table with his ice cream. It was a wonder she wasn't running away. Plus, the more people knew, the more likely someone was going to feel the need to warn her about this latest rumor. Her trust had to be so fragile right now. The truth, even if she believed it, would sound weak.

He pushed the worries away for later and addressed a new subject with Emily. "You're not manning the grill today?"

"The only thing I'm doing today is biding my time in the doghouse."

"What'd you do?"

Emily glanced right and left to check for anyone listening. "I dropped a whole batch of fries on the floor."

"Oh, no."

"Oh, yes," Emily said. "I see chopping onions and cleaning the grease trap in my future."

"Sorry."

She shrugged. "I deserve it."

Paula rolled up next to her with two burgers. "Here you go, honey."

Sebastian took them and looked at Emily. "These aren't the fries you dropped, are they?"

"Not as far as you know," she said with a wink.

Paula shoved her towards some drudgery that they both looked happy about as Sebastian took the food to his table.

"Oh, that smells good," his mom said. She ate a fry and sighed. "Who's the girl behind the counter?"

"Emily Mayor."

"I don't think I know that name."

"She moved here about a year ago," Sebastian said. "I know her from the group at church."

His mom nodded. "I thought you two looked friendly."

"She's engaged," he said, in case his mom had any ideas.

"Good for her," she said. "I meant friendly when I said friendly. I know Ella's the one for you."

He took a huge bite of his burger to inhibit the conversation.

"It's just nice to see that you do have friends in town. Not everyone believes you capable of..." Her sweater covered her arms because of the air conditioning. She tugged on a sleeve. "Ella won't believe it either."

Sebastian continued to chew, though the flavor wasn't quite as satisfying as usual.

"Do you want me to explain things to her?" his mom asked.

"No, Mom." He put down his food. "Do not explain anything to anyone."

"I'll just casually tell her about –"

"No," he said again. "Sebastian didn't do anything. I'm only black and blue because... Don't you hear how defensive and guilty that sounds to bring up out of the blue?"

"It sounds like the truth to me." She calmly stuck another fry in her mouth.

He only shook his head. He didn't feel like eating anymore. Maybe he needed to give up, to leave Ella alone. Everyone would be telling her to fear him. How could she not doubt under that kind of pressure? She would hate that kind of attention. Any time he spent with her would only add to it.

"Fine," his mom said. "I'll stay out of it. But you're so terrified she won't trust you enough that you can't see you're the one not giving her enough credit."

12

" **O** kay, on three," Ruth said. "One, two, three."

Ella chose paper. She lost. "Now the one that counts," she said. They were playing two out of three. Ella wanted pizza, but she wasn't going to be terribly disappointed if Ruth's pick of burgers won.

Ruth counted again.

Ella lost again. She sighed dramatically, which made Ruth laugh and wave. The loser had to go get the food. Ella grabbed her purse and stood in the doorway to her dad's office. "I'm going to pick up our lunch, all right?"

He nodded. "You lost, huh?"

"I'll be back in a few minutes."

He also laughed and waved.

Burger Brothers wasn't more than two blocks down Main Street so it was a quick trip. She and Ruth had played Rock, Paper, Scissors over the task a few weeks earlier because it was raining. They kept it up just for fun.

Ella squinted until she got her sunglasses out of her purse. Some of her glasses darkened automatically so it took her a few seconds to remember she needed to do something even though she was wearing contacts. She was looking ahead to Burger Brothers when she realized she was passing Granny's Shelf. The bunny.

She'd forgotten all about it. She stopped at the window and looked over the various items.

She thought the bunny had been right at eye level. Was she remembering wrong or was it not there anymore? It was definitely nowhere in the window display. Ella would have shrugged off the disappointment and moved on except that it occurred to her that Mrs. Johnson might have put it back for her. She had said she would return for it later. She didn't want the nice old woman to think she'd only been making an excuse not to buy it before.

Nervously, Ella pulled open the door and faced the extreme quiet of the store. Her footsteps exposed her as the only thing moving or making noise. Mrs. Johnson appeared from behind a shelf so suddenly that Ella jumped.

The old lady smiled. "Can I help you find something?"

"I, uh... I don't know if you remember, but I was in a few weeks ago to look at a glass bunny over there."

"Of course I remember."

"I don't see it in the window anymore," Ella said. "Do you still have it?"

A look of confusion passed briefly across her face before she said, "I thought... I'm afraid I sold that not long after you were in."

"Oh." Maybe Ella should have asked her to save it. She'd been so flustered by Sebastian's entrance. "I don't suppose you'd have any idea where to find another one like it?"

"I'm sorry, dear. Most of what I sell I've picked up at estate sales and thrift stores."

Estate sales? There was actually a chance that bunny was the same one that used to sit on her grandmother's end table. She should have come back for it sooner.

"I really am sorry." Mrs. Johnson seemed to be picking up on her distress. "I wouldn't give up hope though," she said. "It might just end up in your hands yet. Some of these went through several owners before they came to me, and God can… He might surprise you."

"That's okay," Ella said. She didn't want to make the woman feel bad for something that wasn't her fault. She had every right to make a sale. "Thanks for letting me look around a bit." She smiled brightly, though possibly too brightly to be believable, before she exited the shop.

Her stomach rumbled to refocus Ella on her destination. They had gotten to lunch a bit late. Paula was cleaning a table when she entered. Ella almost didn't recognize her because she moved at a regular pace when she turned to greet Ella.

"Hello," Ella said. Without the skates, Paula was only about an inch taller. That made her seem closer and just different. "No skates?"

"Ha! Number eight," Paula yelled towards the kitchen as she pointed at Ella. Some people at a nearby table laughed, and Ella felt her face heating up. Paula turned back to explain. "Chip and I have a bet going about how long it will take to have ten people ask about the skates. Two more and I get to put them back on. Thanks."

She walked towards another table at a normal, yet somehow completely unnatural pace. Chip was already waiting for Ella behind the register.

She rushed up, greeted him with a nod, and said, "Two standard cheeseburgers to go, please."

Chip backed enough to give himself room for a slow clap. "That's how you place an order, people." He seemed to be talking to no one in particular but loud enough for everyone to hear.

Ella could feel all eyes in the restaurant on her back as she paid. Sometimes she wished she wasn't so invisible, but most of the time she preferred to stay as unnoticed as possible. The burning on her cheeks was why. She planned to give Ruth an earful about this visit while they ate.

She stepped over to the pickup window and peeked inside. It was too early for Emily to be working. She saw Luke by the grill. The place smelled good and piqued her hunger. It didn't take long before Chip was wrapping up her burgers.

Luke brought them to the window. "Got your order," he said. He made no move to hand it to her. She feared yet another bout of nonstandard interaction.

"Thanks," she said.

"Look. I hear you've been getting friendly with Sebastian Jones."

The fact that Ella was turning red *again* gave her away so she went ahead and nodded.

"You need to stay away from him before you get hurt," Luke said. "The guy's beating his own mother now."

"What!?"

"I figured you hadn't heard." He leaned a bit closer to the window. "She's been black and blue more than once. Several people saw her at bingo recently with a bruise on her arm shaped just like a handprint. Cops were even out there this week to investigate."

Ella stared at him in disbelief. She felt in her gut that Sebastian would never do something like that. But was it possible that someone else was hurting his mom? What was going on? All she knew at the moment was that what was probably meant as well-meaning advice felt like an attack. She said, "Okay," which didn't really make sense. She only wanted to end the scene and get out of there.

"Sorry to upset you," Luke said as he handed over her lunch. "Just want you to be careful."

She nodded. But she turned back before she left. "I think you're wrong," she said. There was power in her voice that she hardly recognized. "I don't know why you're so quick to believe everything you hear about Sebastian. He's one of the nicest people I know, and you... you are *wrong*." Then she got herself and her burgers out of the restaurant as fast as she could.

Back on the sidewalk, there was no one in sight. And no one to watch her quake. She wanted to talk to Sebastian about this, just to make sure his mom was okay. But how could she ask him? Wouldn't it sound like an accusation? Wouldn't it suggest she believed he might have hurt his mom? There was no way he did that. She'd seen the two of them together. She'd seen the way his mom would rather cling to his arm than use a walker. She clearly wasn't afraid of him. And Ella had seen the look on his face when his mom stumbled. This story wasn't true.

When Ella returned to work with the food, Ruth's eyes widened at the sight of her. "Hey, Mr. Sweet?" she called. "Ella's back. We're going to eat on the bench, okay?"

"I'll let you know if I need you," came the reply.

Ruth grabbed a water bottle from her desk and another from Ella's and motioned her back out the door with a tip of her head.

They walked to what they considered their bench only ten feet or so from the front door. Ruth traded a water bottle for a burger as they sat down. She set the burger in her lap. "All right," she said. "Tell me why you look like you've seen a ghost."

Ella was still a bit dazed. She blew out a breath. "I, um, I got the burgers from Luke, and he said he heard I've been seeing Sebastian."

"Oh?" Ruth looked interested.

"He said... he warned me not to get involved with him."

Now Ruth looked confused. She began to unwrap her burger. "That's hardly surprising," she said. "We both know there's no love lost between those two."

"Yeah, but... he said... it was so specific." Ella leaned closer and lowered her voice. "He said Sebastian's been accused of abusing his mom. He said there was even one on her arm shaped like a handprint. The police went to their house to investigate and everything."

"Oh, my goodness." Ruth covered her mouth with both hands. She looked more upset than Ella felt.

"You don't think he could've..."

"No!" Ruth cut her off.

Ella hadn't intended to finish the thought anyway.

"I know he didn't," Ruth said. "It was me."

"What?" Ella didn't understand at all. "What do you mean?"

"Do you remember when I came to help you set up the gym for bingo, and Sebastian's mom almost fell?"

"Yeah."

"But I caught her arm?"

"Yeah."

"That's when it happened," Ruth said. "I was talking to her after we got everything ready, and I noticed a bruise on her arm that I didn't think had been there before. It was right where I'd grabbed her so I asked if I had done that because... I mean, I didn't think I'd been that rough, but maybe... it happened fast and all. Anyway, she told me that she bruises really easily. It's a side effect of her medication. She pushed up her sleeve and showed me two other bruises. She said one was from barely bumping a doorway, and she didn't even know how she got the other one. She laughed at how the mark I'd left already had lines from the fingers and assured me that it didn't hurt at all. She said it was better than what might have happened if she'd hit the floor so I shouldn't worry about it so I didn't. I didn't give it another thought." She put her hand over her mouth again. "It didn't occur to me that Sebastian could get blamed for it."

"Wow." Ella felt great relief at knowing the truth. "I'm actually glad it was you," she said. "Now I don't have to ask Sebastian. I only would've wanted to make sure his mom was okay, but he might've thought I suspected... that I suspected *him*."

"I'm glad you're glad," Ruth said. "But I feel a little sick. Can you imagine having the police show up to question you about abusing your mom?"

Ella winced. That would have been terrible. It was another reason she didn't want to bring it up with him. She imagined Sebastian's mom handling it though. "I bet she got them straightened out pretty quickly," she said. "She doesn't strike me as a woman to pull any punches, and the medication could be verified by her doctor."

"I guess." Ruth nodded slowly. "I wonder if I should apologize."

"For catching her?"

"No, I... I could have explained what happened to more than... I think I told Gabe about it, and that's it."

Ella's mood lightened a bit more as she finally enjoyed a taste of her cheeseburger. "You should have fought gossip with more gossip?" she asked.

Ruth sighed. "I guess that's not the answer." She bit into her burger as well. "I should still maybe tell Sebastian I'm sorry he got blamed. Unless you think he'd rather forget it?"

"I don't know," Ella said. "I'd like to forget how I told Luke off."

"You did what?" Ruth seemed caught between surprise and laughter.

"I kind of yelled at him. I don't know what came over me, but... It was a bad trip all around. Chip clapped at my order and Paula –"

The door to the insurance office opened, and Ella saw her dad's head appear. "Ella," he said, "there's a phone call for you."

"For me?" She left her lunch on the bench as she walked towards the door.

"Yeah, I asked if I could help, and she said it was personal." He held the door wide for her to enter ahead of him.

Ella went to her desk and picked up her phone. "This is Ella," she said.

"Hi, Ella. It's Teresa Jones."

Ella sat down. Why was Sebastian's mom calling her? There was no possible way the woman could know she'd just been talking about her, but she felt guilty nonetheless. "What can I do for you?" She tried to use her business voice even though she knew it wasn't a business call.

"Are you planning on going to the young adult meeting at the church tonight?" she asked.

"Yes."

"Great! That doesn't start until eight o'clock. I thought you might like to come to the house and have dinner with me and Sebastian beforehand."

"Dinner? What time?" Ella asked about the time before she processed what a terrible idea this was. Some instinct told her that Sebastian didn't know anything about this phone call. He was taking things so slowly she still had doubts about his level of interest. How upset would he be when he found out his mom was playing matchmaker? Would he mind that Ella went along with it, or would he perhaps be happy to see her? If Ella turned down the invitation, would Sebastian never find out about it? She really wanted to see him though. Then again, she'd already ambushed him once.

"I don't think we'll eat until about 6:30," Ms. Jones said. "But you could come over earlier."

Yes or no? Yes or no? Ella knew what she wanted to say, but she didn't know if she should.

13

Sebastian put the cutting board in the sink and washed his hands. He turned back to the pan to stir the diced chicken. The pieces sizzled as he moved them around.

His mom stepped into the kitchen. She was still carrying the walker around, but she'd been true to her word as far as having it with her so he didn't complain. "Smells good," she said.

"Thanks." Not that he could really take credit for the way chicken smelled. "We just had this last week. I don't know why you wanted to have it again so soon."

She smiled oddly. Odd because it looked guilty, and he hadn't been seriously suggesting there was anything wrong with eating something she liked again.

"Is there actually a reason behind this request?" he asked.

"Well, I know we had a fair amount of leftovers last time."

"You want leftovers?" he asked doubtfully. There was something suspicious in the way she said it.

"That's how I knew it was a recipe large enough for… say, an extra person or two."

Sebastian put down the spatula and narrowed his eyes at her. "Mom, why do we need enough for an extra person or two?"

"I may have invited someone to join us." She tacked on an innocent smile.

"You may have or you did?"

"I invited Ella."

"What?" He picked up the spatula again and shoved the chicken more forcefully than before. "I thought you were going to stay out of it."

"I said I wouldn't tell her anything you didn't want me to tell her," she said. "There's nothing wrong with trying to get to know her a bit."

"Wait a minute." He nearly dropped the spatula. "Did she actually agree to come over?"

His mom chuckled at the surprise. "Oh, she's so sweet. I think she was as afraid to say no as she was afraid to say yes. But somehow yes won out."

"What time are you expecting her?"

"Pretty soon," she said with a glance at her watch. "I told her dinner wouldn't be ready yet."

"What made you think this was a good idea?"

She shrugged. "Someone needed a plan, and you won't admit to having one."

"This isn't a plan, Mom. It's just… sad."

"Is it sad that Ella apparently wanted to come over here to see you?"

"I didn't invite her," he said. "Maybe she wants to see you." He was only arguing to give his mom a hard time, but he wondered if that was why Ella agreed to visit. Maybe she wanted to see how much his mom feared him to know how much she should.

His mom was eyeing him as though she was trying to read his thoughts.

"What?" he asked.

"Do you want to know the rest of the plan or not?"

Sebastian turned off the burner and opened a cupboard to grab a few ingredients to distract himself. Otherwise, he might have asked about the plan he didn't want to know anything about. When he glanced back at his mom, she appeared to be still waiting for an answer. "Mom, when you talk about having a plan," he said, "it sounds like you're trying to manipulate her."

"Nonsense." She waved a hand to dismiss his remark. "I figure I'll bring her in here to sit at the table so we can chat while you're cooking."

"Fine." That wasn't a plan. It was simply common sense to have this chat where he could supervise it.

"That way you can listen and maybe learn a few things yourself. If you think I'm being too nosy, you can drop a pan or something."

He opened a lower cupboard and pulled out a stack of about a half dozen pans. He set it on the counter and said, "This should get us started."

"Ha!" His mom nearly doubled over. "My baby is a comedian," she said. "I'll tell Ella about that. Women love a sense of humor."

"I wasn't kidding," he said. "Also, you can add trying to sell her on me having a sense of humor to the list of things you're not allowed to talk about."

She rolled her eyes at him.

"In fact, don't talk about me at all."

The doorbell rang. Sebastian took a step towards the door.

His mom stopped him with a raised hand. "My guest," she said. "I'll get the door."

He looked at the recipe to see if he was forgetting anything. It was difficult to concentrate when he could hear his mom greeting Ella with way too much enthusiasm. The walker entered the kitchen first, actually rolling on the ground. Sebastian involuntarily wondered how that fit into the plan.

Ella came in behind his mom. Her eyes darted nervously around the room and bounced off him before they came back with a small smile. "Hi," she said.

Her hair seemed longer all of a sudden. Maybe he'd only seen it curly a lot lately. She was wearing light blue and looked soft and fragile. "Hi, Ella."

"You can sit here." Sebastian's mom directed Ella to a chair at the table that let her face him. Then she moved herself to the corner. "Someone over there is going to be making dinner while we talk, but I'm not allowed to mention him."

A smile twitched across Ella's face. "Did he give you a list?"

"That's exactly what he said." His mom lowered herself into her chair as she spoke in what was apparently supposed to sound like Sebastian's voice. "Here's the list of things you're not allowed to talk about. I'm at the top."

"Does this count?" Ella asked.

She looked at Sebastian, then back at Ella. "He's not making a lot of noise to drown me out so I think we're okay so far."

Ella looked at Sebastian, too. He realized he was just standing there watching them talk, staring at Ella really. He kept his ears open but shifted his attention to the task of not ruining dinner.

"How long have you worked for your dad?"

"Since I finished college," Ella said. "So just barely over four years."

"Does that make you twenty-six?"

Sebastian looked up to see Ella nod. "I remember your birthday was a Friday," he said. "Ruth made everyone in the group sing to you, but I don't think you really appreciated it."

"I'm not a fan of the spotlight," Ella said, "but I did appreciate the thought."

Sebastian's mom turned to him and said, "Don't interrupt."

Ella seemed to find that amusing. She wiped it away quickly to prepare for the next question.

"Did you always plan to work for your dad?"

"Not exactly. Or not really." Ella paused to think. "I didn't know what I wanted to do when I was in school. About a year before I graduated, my dad asked how I'd feel about it. The woman who used to work for him was talking about retiring. He wondered if it'd be a good idea to convince her to stay long enough to train me. She liked the plan, too, and… I don't know. It worked out great though."

"When you say you didn't know what you wanted to do, you mean as a job?"

Sebastian looked up as Ella nodded. She looked as wary as he was about where that question might be leading.

"Was part of you hoping to meet a man instead?" his mom asked.

Sebastian moved the stack of pans along the counter to try to get his mom's attention. Either it didn't work, or she ignored him.

But Ella didn't seem to mind the question. "I don't know about instead," she said. "But I won't deny I was keeping my eyes open for prospects."

"Are your eyes still open?"

"Mom?" Sebastian said, trying to sound calm and casual.

When she turned to him, he picked up one of those empty pans. "Where do you want me to put this?"

She snorted and waved off the question.

Ella looked between them as though she knew she was missing something.

"You are still hoping to get married?" His mom pressed the question to Ella.

"Yeah, I still hope…" She didn't seem to mind answering,

but she was turning pink. Her eyes made contact with Sebastian's for barely a second before they found the table. "Someday," she quickly added.

Did she tack on that word to clarify that they weren't serious enough to be talking about a wedding or did she mean someday after she met someone who didn't scare her? Ella had basically asked him the same question a week ago. Was she uncomfortable now because his mom was in the room or because she'd been hearing things about how he treated his mom?

Black beans, chili powder… Sebastian read the ingredients to himself a few times to banish the distracting thoughts. He mixed up some cornbread batter and poured it on top before sticking it in the oven. The other side of the kitchen was very quiet as he closed the oven door. He was aware that it had been quiet for a while and began to realize that might not be better than probing questions.

Ella had her elbows on the table and her hands folded in front of her mouth. His mom said something to her with her voice deliberately low. He couldn't make it out from the side. Ella's eyes lit up as though whatever it was made her smile. She glanced at him but quickly looked away again.

Sebastian was struck by how odd the scene was. He was no stranger to people whispering in his presence. But most people acted as though he was oblivious. Ella looked as though she couldn't wait for him to notice. Another glance drew him to the table like a magnet.

His mom said something that might have been, "Let's wait until he asks," or "Don't say it until he asks."

Ella responded with something too mumbled for him to guess. They both smiled and deliberately avoided looking his way as he sat down. It probably should have felt good to see these two women he cared about getting along, but there was something unnerving about it. It sort of felt as though they didn't need him.

"Dinner will be ready in about fifteen minutes," he said.

Ella put her hands down and nodded at him. "It smells good," she said.

"Thanks," he said. But again, chicken smelled good. All he did was put it in a pan.

"He's making one of my favorites," his mom said. "Sebastian knows his way around the kitchen."

He gestured to the fairly small space by the counter. "Hard to get lost over there."

"For all his strengths, he still can't take a compliment."

"I thought we agreed we weren't going to be talking about me at all tonight," Sebastian said.

"No one agreed to anything," his mom retorted. "You told me I wasn't allowed to." She looked at Ella. "It wasn't that long ago that I got to make the rules around here."

Ella nodded with a sympathetic expression, as though she agreed that Sebastian was being completely unreasonable.

It didn't matter how unreasonable he was or if he'd only been kidding because his mom ignored him. She said, "When I told him I asked you over for dinner, he asked me why I thought that was a good idea."

"It sounds terrible when you say it like that, Mom."

The smug look on her face told him she knew that and enjoyed putting him on the spot to explain. And he needed to explain because Ella was trying not to appear hurt.

"She waited until ten minutes before you got here to say anything," he said. "I was asking why she thought it was a good idea to be sneaky about it. I mean, what if I wasn't making enough food?"

"I'm sorry," Ella said.

"What? No. It's not your fault." He didn't understand why that had made her apologize.

"She didn't call me until this afternoon," Ella said. "I should have known that would be too short notice."

"It's just dinner." Sebastian's mom reached out and patted Ella's hand. An ugly purple mark poked out of her sleeve. "We have dinner every day. We only need notice for special occasions. Unless Sebastian thought your visit was special enough to need notice?"

Sebastian was distracted by that bruise on her arm, torn between asking his mom to cover it back up and knowing there was nothing to hide. If Ella believed he might do that, the fear would be there whether anything purple was visible or not. As he got his thoughts back to the conversation, he realized his mom was staring at him and Ella was staring at the table. They were both waiting for him to confirm what they both already knew. According to Emily, everyone knew it.

It wasn't that it was supposed to be a secret. He was afraid that any kind of declaration of his intentions would force a response from Ella. He did not want to put pressure on her. Then again, she'd agreed to come over when she had to know his mom was playing matchmaker. Even if she had been afraid to say no, yes had won. Maybe she was ready to respond.

"Maybe I just wanted to be the one to invite her," he said.

"Great." His mom clapped her hands and startled whatever reaction Ella might have had right out of her. "You can invite her over again on Sunday." She turned to Ella. "If you're going to help with bingo and not stay to play, you gotta come get some dinner to make it worth your time."

Ella opened her mouth to protest.

Sebastian's mom was faster. "Don't answer now," she said.

"Sebastian will talk you into it later." Then she turned to her son. "Go get the cards."

"What cards?" he asked. He probably knew what cards. It was an instinctual response to her very sudden request.

She rolled her eyes, presumably because she knew he knew what cards. "The cards for playing games," she said. "We'll teach her to play Openers."

"We don't have time to play that before dinner."

"We don't have time to play, but we have time to teach." She waved him towards the living room. "Then we'll be ready to play as soon as we're done eating."

Sebastian looked at Ella. "How do you feel about learning a card game?"

"Okay." There was an eagerness in her eyes that didn't match her tone. He believed she was a little nervous but not just being polite.

Most likely she was relieved by the thought of talking about something as impersonal as numbers and suits for a while. The conversation stayed neutral over dinner as well. Sebastian's mom continued to pump Ella for information, but she asked about foods and movies she liked and what she studied in school. The topics were reasonably safe. Then they played some cards. Ella caught on quickly, which wasn't a surprise since he knew she was smart and had said she liked games.

The game ended just in time for Sebastian and Ella to leave for the meeting at church, though in truth they were rushing a bit to make that happen. His mom reminded him – in front of Ella – that he was in charge of inviting her back on Sunday.

Ella's car was parked behind his in the driveway.

"It seems like a waste to take two cars when we're going the same place," he said. "But there's no way to do it without you having to come back out here and since you live closer to the church…"

"Yeah, I'll…" She fidgeted as though she was changing her mind about what to say. "I'll see you there." And then she was already moving towards her car.

Sebastian drove behind her. There were only two other cars in the lot when they pulled in so it was easy to keep track of hers. She didn't seem in a hurry to get out. He thought she might be checking messages or something. Rather than hover, Sebastian moved towards the entrance to wait for her there.

Another car parked while he waited. Heather got out of the driver's side and another woman was with her. She wasn't a regular, but she was familiar. That was normal in a town the size of Andauk. He thought she might be the sister of someone he went to school with. She and Heather whispered to each other as they approached. Furtive glances toward the door did not suggest to him they were talking about the door.

It didn't feel as though people gossiped about him very often at these meetings anymore. They'd gotten used to him or at least the fact that he was willing to show his face. But this new woman changed something, or maybe the new story did. He held the door for the two of them, trying to smile as though he hadn't noticed the whispering. Heather mumbled a thank you. The other woman tried to hide behind Heather as she slipped past.

A sudden desire sparked to skip the meeting, to take Ella somewhere else. He wanted to keep hoping she hadn't yet heard the rumor that would shake her trust, to believe just a little while longer that she might convince herself not to be afraid of Sebastian Jones.

14

Ella sat in her car for a few minutes trying to pull herself together. She was so tired. It wasn't a sleepy kind of tired. It was only 8 o'clock after all. But she'd just spent two hours trying to make a good impression on Ms. Jones when every instinct made her want to run for the door. Sebastian had been upset with his mom for inviting her. He'd tried to act as though it wasn't a big deal, but Ella wasn't stupid. She saw that it wasn't what he wanted.

For so long she'd been telling herself that he kept a respectful distance because of his reputation, that he was chasing her slowly to give her time to trust him. But they'd cleared the air. They'd had a few good long talks. She'd foolishly agreed to an obvious ploy by his mom. She'd practically prostrated herself at his feet, and he'd realized it wasn't what he wanted. She wasn't what he wanted. His eyes had practically burned a hole in his mom when she talked about having Ella over again.

She got out of her car trying to still her nerves. Sebastian was waiting for her. He was still trying to be polite. Maybe it was the exhaustion that made her desperate, but she wanted one more chance. She wanted a little more time to prove that even though she was shy and skittish at first, that didn't mean she was boring.

"Hey, Ella," he said as she got close. "I have a crazy idea."

She listened expectantly. She was absolutely in the mood for a crazy idea.

"Do you want to play hooky?" He bit the side of his lip as though he doubted it and his eyes... oh, wow, his eyes.

"Yes," she said.

"Really?"

She nodded and motioned him to follow her. She hadn't the faintest idea where she was leading him. She only knew she wanted to get out of there before anyone saw them and asked where they were going. They went several blocks in silence, almost at a jog.

Ella stopped as they came alongside a chain-link fence. It surrounded the jr. high football field and looked about eight feet high. "I wonder if I could climb this fence," she said aloud.

"I think you could," Sebastian said.

She shook her head. Whatever emotion made her want to run also made her want to try to scale the fence. But she doubted she was physically capable. She'd probably fall on her face or get to the top and be too scared to go over.

"I believe you could," Sebastian insisted, "but that it would be a waste of effort because it's open on that side." He pointed closer to the school.

He was right. She'd known the fence didn't go all the way around but was thinking only of climbing, not of getting somewhere. Now the bleachers she saw by the opening felt like a destination. She jogged towards them.

Her footsteps echoed on the metal steps with no one else around. No one except Sebastian, whose footsteps echoed behind hers. He followed her to the top row where he sat on the other side of the center steps.

"Sebastian, I'm sorry," she said suddenly.

His throat jumped as he swallowed. "Why are you sorry?"

"Because I knew your mom didn't ask you before she invited me over," she said. "I shouldn't have ambushed you again."

"It wasn't an…" He stopped his automatic protest as he realized what she said. "What do you mean again?"

Ella felt as though she had nothing to lose by admitting everything. "At the Ice Cream Shack. Ruth and I set you up."

"You did?" His eyes moved around as he searched his memory for exactly what had happened that day.

"She sat with us so no one else could, but she planned to move. It was just lucky that Adam came in and gave her an easy excuse."

"I'm not sure I understand."

"I wanted to get you alone but not completely alone to ask about… Kathy, in case…" The sentence was too awful to finish. Sitting by that empty field with Sebastian, Ella was sure she felt safer than she would have if she was alone. "Ruth thought it was a good idea," she added, which was true even if she hadn't been the only one.

Sebastian nodded. He understood the part she didn't say. He looked saddened by it but not offended. "As long as you're admitting things," he said, "what were you and my mom whispering about before dinner?"

"Oh." Ella laughed. "That was… she just kept saying stuff like, if I whisper, he'll come over here and yell at me for talking about him."

Sebastian sighed. "That sounds like something she'd do."

It suddenly occurred to Ella how wrong it had been to whisper in front of someone who was constantly whispered about. "I'm sorry," she said.

He shifted nervously on the bench. "Now why are you sorry?"

"For the… It was rude to make you think we were talking

about you. Especially given how often people actually... you know."

"I do know," he said. "But that's different. You and my mom were just teasing. I didn't mind."

She believed that he didn't mind. In fact, the way he looked at her when he said it made her think that what he really didn't mind was sitting there next to her. Except that he wasn't next to her. If she stuck her arm straight out, she'd still have to lean over to reach his shoulder. She still wanted to believe he was attracted to her, but she could only tell herself he was moving slowly so many times before she wondered if he was trying to move at all. Maybe he only wanted a friend, someone who would vouch for him when he found the girl he did want.

The thought made it impossible for Ella to sit still. She stood up and threw one leg over the seat in front of her to walk lopsided towards the other end.

"Ella?" Sebastian sounded confused.

She didn't blame him because he wasn't the only one. She turned around and clomped back towards him with the other leg higher. If he got her alone to let her down easy, he should get it over with. "I'm sorry," she said. "I'm just... antsy all of a sudden. Why didn't you want to go to the meeting tonight?"

He shrugged. "I had a sudden impulse to avoid people."

"But not me?"

"No." He smiled only faintly. "You're not *people*."

"I'll take that as a compliment," Ella said. She also thought crowds could be draining. Even a group of people she liked.

She grabbed the bar along the back and peered behind the bleachers. "I remember being at the top of some bleachers like this with my brother once. It wasn't here, it was... at the county fair I think. Anyway, the seats were very full, and my brother — he must have been about nine or ten – he climbed right down the back instead of… I guess he just didn't want to have to say excuse me to the whole line of people. Of course, I had to in order to follow him. I was supposed to be watching him."

She pushed herself back and regarded Sebastian. The sun was low, but it hadn't really begun to set. She could see clearly that he was looking back at her somewhat curiously. Perhaps it was because she'd never held eye contact so long with him. Something about the night or the strong feelings creeping up on her or the impulse to run away from their regular plans… something was making her braver than usual. But perhaps he only looked curious because she hadn't gotten to the point of her random story. "I can't picture you doing anything like that."

"Like what?"

"Do you know the movie *It's a Wonderful Life?*"

"I've seen it a few times," he said. "My mom loves it."

"There's a scene where George is talking to his dad about his brother taking over his job at the same age George started and the dad says, 'You were born older.'" Ella paused to see if Sebastian had any idea what she meant.

He nodded. "I think I remember that scene."

"For some reason, that's what I'm thinking about you. I'm trying to picture you running around like a little boy, and I'm thinking you were somehow born older than the rest of us."

"It sounds like…" Sebastian sort of frowned at her. "It kind of sounds like you're trying to accuse me of being no fun."

"No, that's not it." Ella clunked down a row and moved around to sit on Sebastian's other side, only a little closer than they were before. Then she stood up again. "Just more mature. Kids and grownups have different fun. You…" He was fun. She enjoyed all the time she'd spent with him. She liked him. It wasn't fear that kept her from saying any of those things. It was the fact that they wouldn't be taken seriously at the moment. Sebastian looked far too amused by her explanation.

"Different fun? That's the most interesting way I've ever been called boring. But I'd like to point out that you're the one who brought us out here to watch an imaginary football game." He raised his arm towards the empty field. "Go team!"

Ella laughed and looked out at the open space. Trees along the edge cast long shadows like stripes across the grass. A few June bugs gathered under a streetlight that had barely flickered to life. Though the evening was warm, she felt a slight shiver.

"Are you cold?" Sebastian asked.

She shook her head because it wasn't the temperature that made her shiver but some sort of anticipation in the air. Was she the only one who felt it? Then she almost regretted the honesty. Because if she said she was cold, it would be an excuse to sit closer, to see if he'd put an arm around her.

"Sebastian?" She turned around to ask him a question that she immediately forgot. The spell of being alone was broken by the sight of an old man running towards them. "Is that Jojo?" she asked instead.

Sebastian turned around, then nodded. He got up and stomped down the stairs to meet Jojo. He didn't really stomp; his feet were loud on the steps because the steps were loud. Ella followed slowly and stayed a few steps from the bottom to let Sebastian talk to him.

Jojo stopped in front of the bleachers and worked to catch his breath.

"Hey, Jojo," Sebastian said. "Is everything all right?"

The man noticed Ella and straightened briefly before dipping into a graceful bow.

She nodded a greeting at him.

He turned away from both of them and held his hand above his eyes though there was no sun to shield them from.

"Are you looking for something?" Sebastian asked.

Jojo began to hurry away as though he hadn't heard. But then he came back. He unbuttoned the front of his shirt. Judging by the colors at the hem, he was wearing at least three more when he took off the first one. He wrapped the sleeves around his waist and tied them so firmly Ella heard a small tearing sound. He stuck his tongue out and made a panting sound. Ella thought he was saying he was hot.

But Sebastian said, "A dog? Are you looking for a dog?"

Jojo nodded vigorously.

"I didn't know you had a dog."

Jojo pointed. He wasn't looking that way and didn't seem to be pointing at anything in particular.

"Is it someone else's dog?" Sebastian asked.

More vigorous nodding.

"What does it look like?"

Jojo tugged on his various sleeves until he found something blue and white checked.

"White?" Sebastian asked, which was the first guess that didn't impress Ella. She wasn't keeping up with the conversation as well as he was, but there weren't a lot of blue dogs.

The old man leaned over to hold his hand above the ground.

"Pretty small?" Sebastian interpreted. "Oh. Doesn't your sister have a dog like that?"

His eyes widened, and he nodded again.

"Okay. We haven't seen it, but we'll keep our eyes open." Sebastian turned to Ella. "I think it's a Yorkie mix. Small, white and kind of shaggy."

"Should we help him look for it?" she asked.

Sebastian shrugged. "I think if the dog's wandering around town, we'd be just as likely to spot it staying put as we would if we were also wandering."

She thought that made sense. But she wanted to stay where she was so she had to admit that made her easy to convince.

Sebastian waved at Jojo's retreating back. The man had started running away about as abruptly as he'd shown up.

"Did you have a dog when you were a kid?" Ella asked.

"No."

"Did you want one?"

"No," he said. "I mean, I don't dislike dogs or anything. I just... I guess no one ever convinced me it would be worth the effort."

She was still three steps off the ground, and it felt strange to look down when she talked to someone significantly taller than she was. "This is a weird perspective," she said.

"Um..." His brow furrowed. "You're not talking about dogs anymore, are you?"

"I'm sorry." She came down a step and shrunk slightly by comparison. "I'm all over the place tonight." She really was. Between the changing topics and the fidgeting, her nerves were covering a lot of ground.

Sebastian didn't say anything. He sort of looked as though he was waiting for her to finish talking.

Ella sat on the bench behind her and put her feet on the one in front of her. She stared at her shoes. They were just shoes. They couldn't give her what she wanted, which was some sort of confirmation that Sebastian was interested in a possible future with her. She thought he might be. Sometimes he looked at her like there was nothing in the world he wanted more. But he never said or did anything that specifically confirmed it.

"Are you okay?" he asked after a minute. The metal creaked as he sat down. He sat at the bottom with his feet still on the ground. If anything, he was farther than when he was standing. Even a friend would take a step closer if he thought she might need comfort. Right?

Ella gathered the courage she'd been alternately embracing and tripping over. "Your mom said something about inviting me over again," she said. "What did you think of that?"

"I think she made a suggestion I didn't need."

"Because you... you already want to see me more often?" There. Ella exhaled. The question was out there. It had clear romantic undertones. All he had to do was say yes.

His expression was apologetic, which nearly turned her stomach inside out until he said, "I didn't hear what you just said."

Apparently, the courage didn't quite reach her timid vocal cords. She stood up again and walked along the metal to let its clanging take the place of talking for a few seconds. When she turned around, Sebastian was also standing, waiting where she'd started. She walked back. "I'm sorry," she said. She knew it would have been easier to just repeat herself. "People always tell me to speak up, but I don't always know when I'm being too quiet."

"Ella, please..." He ran both hands through his hair.

"Please what?"

"Do you know how many times you've apologized tonight? Please don't say you're sorry unless... You're making me so nervous."

She could feel the tension in his voice but didn't understand it. "How does that make you nervous?" she asked.

"Every time you say I'm sorry, I think you're about to add, but this isn't going to work."

This? Sebastian thought this was something, something he'd be disappointed to end. Now they were almost on the same page. But just to be sure, she said, "You're saying you want this, me and you, you want this to work?"

He gave a short, surprised laugh. "Are you seriously asking me that?"

She nodded. It felt small but bold. She'd asked.

"You really... My mom thinks I'm so pathetic I need her help and I guarantee when we didn't show up tonight, everyone there was like oh, Ella decided to do something else and Sebastian followed her off like a lovesick puppy. But *you* have to ask?"

Not anymore. His sarcasm cleared things up a little too nicely. She got defensive and suddenly bugged by being higher than him. She wanted the normal height difference where she was the smaller one so she stepped to the ground near him. "You didn't say anything before now."

"No, I didn't." And he looked as though he regretted the way he'd said it now. "I didn't want you to have to decide too soon if you could get past... everything."

"You want me to decide something now?"

"No. I don't want to pressure you." He took a step backwards, as if he wasn't already far enough away. "I wouldn't have said anything, but you asked."

"Well, what if... what happens if it's not too soon?"

"Oh." It was more than disappointment, but his expression recovered quickly. "If this is the part where you say I'm sorry for real, I'll do the best I can to make it easy on you. I'll..." He trailed off in response to a lot of head shaking on her part.

"I can't... Not until... I mean, how do you know when it's not too soon if you don't say anything? Or... do anything?"

"Are you saying you'd be okay if…" He moved only a foot forward before he stopped. "You have to be sure, Ella."

"Okay."

"Okay?" He repeated it doubtfully.

She'd answered without thinking and now she wondered if it was the right answer. As badly as she wanted him to come closer, she was so jumpy she wasn't sure she could hold still long enough for a kiss, if that was what he had in mind. Not if she knew it was coming.

Sebastian stared at her for a long moment. He held perfectly still. The leaves stopped rustling and the gathering darkness blotted out everything beyond the field. Ella felt her lungs pumping overtime and that seemed to be the only movement. Was he going to make a move or not?

Finally, she saw his hand out of the corner of her eye. She didn't know if he was reaching for her hand or maybe for her face. Either would have been wonderful. But he pulled back before he made contact. He opened his mouth to say something, but the words seemed to be stuck. Then he gave up and started walking away.

"Sebastian?" She knew her voice was too quiet that time. She'd barely breathed it. Ella sucked in some air and called out. "Sebastian?"

He stopped. He rubbed his hands over his face and turned around as she caught up.

"What's wrong?" she asked.

"You're still afraid of me."

"No, I'm not." She was though. She was afraid of him leaving.

"You don't want to be, but…"

Ella just shook her head because she didn't know how else to disagree.

"I saw you flinch." His voice cracked on the last word. "I need you to believe I won't hurt you and if I have to stay far away to prove it then that's what I have to do." He was backing up even as he spoke and turned away without giving Ella a chance to say anything else.

She watched him go as she rewound the conversation in her head. She'd been too flustered to process it in the moment, but now it made sense. She walked slowly to the church to make sure he was gone when she got to her car. Tears poured down her face, and she didn't want Sebastian to see that. She drove straight home and hoped she could get to her bedroom without her parents noticing either. Naturally, her dad was right there when she came through the door.

"Ella, what's wrong?" he asked, rushing forward.

"Nothing." She waved him off. "Or nothing that... I just need to talk to Ruth."

He winced and seemed to understand it was some sort of emotional thing. "Okay. But if you need me later..." It was a sweet offer because he was clearly reluctant to be involved.

"I know where to find you," she said. Then she went upstairs and closed her door. Ruth would be at the church a few more minutes, then she'd want to talk to Gabriel for a bit. Ella paced for a minute but felt herself getting worked up by it rather than relaxed. She grabbed pajamas and decided a hot shower might help. At least the water washed away the salt on her face.

Her phone was flashing after the shower. She missed two calls from Ruth before a text that read: He finally asked!!

Ella slumped onto her bed. That was great news with impeccably bad timing. She hated to bring Ruth down. Luckily, it was likely nothing would. She returned the call.

"Ella! Did you see?" Ruth was definitely excited.

"I did. Congratulations!"

Ruth was quiet for a moment. "Ella? Is something wrong?"

Either she'd failed at enthusiasm or the crying left her sounding like she had a cold. "I promise I'm happy for you," Ella said. "I had a pretty bad night though."

"What happened? When you and Sebastian were both missing tonight, I figured you were still at his house. Was there a problem at dinner?"

"No, that was okay." Ella didn't know where to start the story. "We, um, we were on our way to the meeting when he suggested we play hooky."

"Aw. He wanted to be alone."

"Actually, I thought it was a bad sign. I thought he wanted to… I don't know… make sure I wasn't getting the wrong idea or something."

"But you said dinner was okay?"

Ella cringed a bit. "Sort of. I don't know. I could tell he was annoyed with his mom for asking me. But that doesn't matter now. We walked over to the jr. high when we got to the church and we were just sitting on the bleachers talking and… I asked… I guess I wanted to know how interested he was…"

"Okay," Ruth said. Her tone said hurry up and get to the good part.

"Well, he definitely cleared up the level of interest."

"Now I'm confused because you say that like he cleared it up in a good way."

"It was good," Ella said. "But then I screwed up so bad."

"What did you do?"

"I…" Ella started crying again out of nowhere. "I just took

too long to figure it out. He was going to… I'm not sure, but I think he was going to kiss me. But then he didn't. He started to leave, just all of a sudden. He accused me of being afraid of him. He said I flinched. I was confused and disappointed and it took me a few seconds to figure out that I must have jumped. I was so nervous I must have gotten startled and didn't realize it and Sebastian thought… he thought that I thought that he was going to, I don't know, grab me or hit me or something." Ella's tears dried up with a surge of anger. "And the more I think about it the more I wonder if maybe I should be offended that he thought that because why would I think that? Why would I think he'd suddenly turn violent in that beautiful moment unless he doesn't think I have any common sense? But I can't be offended because I know people do think that about him and I hurt him and I should have gone after him, but I didn't think I'd be able to explain myself when I was so upset."

"Wow," Ruth said. "I'm sorry."

"Thank you. I wish I could say I feel better just getting it out, but I don't." Ella rubbed her forehead with her free hand. "What do I do?"

"As bad as it sounds, it's still just a misunderstanding. Can't you call him and explain?"

"I don't think he'll answer. He said he was going to stay away from me to prove he won't hurt me."

Ruth sighed. "That only proves he's an idiot."

"And if I leave a message, I'll never know if he listened to it and still didn't believe me or just deleted it."

"Okay." Ruth sounded as though she was thinking. "What about bingo? It'll be just the two of you setting up."

"And his mom," Ella reminded her. "There's no way she wouldn't be able to tell there was something going on. That would be so embarrassing. I can't even…"

"Afterwards," Ruth said. "Maybe you don't set up but wait for him outside to talk."

"And if he walks away?" Ella could picture it, and her chest squeezed at the thought.

"You need to talk to him sometime."

"Says the woman who didn't talk to Gabriel for *four years*."

"Oh, I deserve that," Ruth said.

"I'm still sorry." It was terrible for Ella to take her frustration out on the person trying to help her.

"No, you're right," Ruth said. "I need to remember how hard it is when it's you. What we need is for Sebastian to make the first move. If he called you or came up to you, could you talk to him then?"

"I think so."

"Good. Okay." Ruth was thinking again. The sound of wheels turning was nearly audible. "I bet I can get Isaac to make him do it."

"What? No." Panic hit. "Don't tell anyone what happened!"

"Don't worry," Ruth said, her voice soothing. "I won't give him any details, not even a little bit. I'll only tell him that he needs to make Sebastian talk to you. I'll need to wait until Sunday though. I can be more persuasive in person. And that'll give you and Sebastian a day to calm down and you time to plan out what you want to say."

"I definitely need to figure out what to say," Ella said. "How do I explain that I am completely terrified but not of what he thinks?"

15

The questions were coming. Sebastian had been doing a pretty good job of avoiding his mom, considering how difficult it was to avoid someone who lived in the same house. But he knew he couldn't avoid her forever.

He was chopping lettuce for a taco salad when she came into the kitchen. She didn't bring her puzzle book or sit at the table. She stood behind him, hovering. Perhaps if he let her ask the questions, she would know he wasn't going to talk about it and that would be the end of it.

"Taco salad?" she asked.

He nodded.

"Looks like enough for three."

"I thought I'd take some for lunch tomorrow."

"I take it then that we are not expecting Ella tonight." It was a statement that begged for an explanation.

"No," Sebastian said.

"You didn't invite her or she had other plans?"

"She's not coming."

"You're not going to tell me why?"

"She's just not coming, Mom."

He heard the walker tap the ground as she moved around to stand beside him. "It's awful early for dinner," she observed. "You just finished lunch."

"I'll put it in the fridge when I'm done," he said. "You can eat whenever you want."

"Whenever you're not eating?" She gave him a disapproving look. "I'm trying not to take it personally that my son doesn't want to be in the same room as me."

He rolled his eyes at the lettuce.

"I saw that," she said. "I know you want me to mind my own business, but when you're as much fun to be around as a pile of surly manure, it becomes my business. I'm just curious how long this is going to go on."

Sebastian almost smiled in spite of his sour mood. He couldn't help wondering what made manure surly. "I'll be done in about ten minutes."

His mom made a scoffing noise, which he expected and ignored. She probably expected that. "Are we going to see Ella before bingo tonight?"

He'd been thinking about that. Ella might show up to honor the commitment she'd made to Mrs. Donnelly, but it would be super awkward for her. Sebastian's best idea was to head over earlier than usual to set everything up before she got there, then he'd come back for his mom. The possible hiccup was that Mrs. Donnelly kept a tight schedule. The door to the gym might not be unlocked if he went too early.

"I don't know." He answered his mom truthfully. "But if we happen to run into her, you... can't..."

The stern look on her face made him pause. He probably hadn't seen that expression since he was about ten years old. "Are you about to tell me to ignore her," she asked, "to be as rude to her as you?"

"I –"

She held up a hand to stop his protest.

Since he didn't want to talk anyway, he scooped the lettuce into the bowl and picked up a tomato.

"I don't know what time you got in Friday, but I know it was later than usual. I figured you spent some extra time with Ella until you spent all day Saturday with the personality of dryer lint, *depressed* dryer lint. I assumed there was a little tiff that would blow over soon enough, until I saw Ella at church this morning. Looking very pretty I might add, even with those sad eyes. And you, I'm sure I've never seen anyone so rudely determined to ignore another person. That's how I know this mess is your fault, and you better apologize to her before it's too late."

Sebastian realized he'd only been staring at the tomato while his mom talked. Maybe now that she got it out of her system, she'd leave him alone.

"Well?" she said.

Apparently not. "Well, what?" he asked.

"Why were you ignoring her this morning?"

"I didn't see her." He was being honest. He'd been deliberately avoiding looking around. It would have been painful to see her and remember the way she'd jerked away in fear. He'd only wanted to take her hand, to make what felt like a growing connection tangible. And it had scared her.

"Hogwash," his mom said. "When are you going to apologize to her?"

"I think I'm a little too old for you to be telling me what to do."

"More hogwash. You're never too old to get advice from your mother, especially when it's good advice." She made a nervous hissing sound. "Also, please don't cut yourself. I don't want any blood in my dinner."

There at least was advice he could heed. The agitation was making him a little careless with the knife.

"Are you going to apologize if we see her tonight?" she asked.

"I doubt we'll see her."

She groaned. "Goodness. You weren't even this stubborn as a teenager."

He slid the unevenly chopped tomato into the bowl and began to clean up. His mom stood back to let him work. When he put the lid on dinner and popped it into the fridge, she blocked his path to leave the room.

"Sebastian."

He closed his eyes. She'd dropped the lecture voice so he knew this speech would be worse.

"I know people need to make their own mistakes," she began. "But speaking as a person with more than my share of regrets, I just have to say that it's plain to me that you love her. You'll regret it so much if you let it end over something stupid."

"I know you mean well," he said, sidling past her, "but sometimes we have to accept the things that cannot be changed."

He went into his bedroom and closed the door. He didn't have anything to do in there except hide. Fortunately, he found that Isaac had just texted him. He grabbed his keys and went back out, replying as he walked. "Isaac wants to meet up for some basketball," he told his mom. "I'll be back in time to take you to bingo."

"Good," she said. "Maybe he can talk some sense into you."

Sebastian was thankful to know that wasn't going to happen. Isaac was a good friend. If he brought up Ella at all, he'd drop it the moment he realized it was a sore subject. It felt good to get out of the house. It wasn't as relieving as he hoped, however, because he'd spent enough time walking around town with Ella that even though they hadn't been to the park, it still made him think of her. Maybe there wasn't a place he could stop thinking about Ella.

He took his ball onto the court to try to make a few shots while he waited for Isaac. The happy shouts of children on the nearby equipment filled the air. The courts were deserted. Sebastian didn't think he'd care, but it was still nice that there was no one around to witness his terrible aim.

The wait for Isaac wasn't long. They said hello as Isaac put his ball on the bench. Then there was a weird pause while Isaac looked uncertain about something before he said, "Let's play."

"You don't need to warm up first, old man?" Sebastian tossed the ball to Isaac, who was a year older so he got to give him a hard time about being thirty.

Isaac didn't say anything as he came out to start the game. In fact, he was quieter than normal the whole time they played. Sebastian enjoyed the exercise even though he lost. Isaac had a couple inch height advantage and was very good. There was no shame in losing to him. Sebastian minded even less than usual though because he knew his head wasn't in the game.

He thought they were about to start another game when Isaac tucked the ball under one arm and said, "Look, man, we have to talk about Ella."

Sebastian just stared at him. He hadn't actually said that, had he?

"Well, *we* don't need to talk, but you need to talk to her."

His head was shaking, more in disbelief at the situation than because he was saying no to anything.

"I thought you were pretty crazy about her."

"What are you doing?" Sebastian asked.

Isaac sighed and rolled his eyes. "Yeah, I don't want to be

involved and the only way I get *un*involved is if you go talk to Ella so can you just say you'll do it?"

"No. Let's play."

"Ruth is mad at me because she's convinced herself it's my fault Ella got hurt."

"I did *not* —"

"Whoa!" Isaac put both hands up defensively and dropped the ball. "I didn't mean that," he said. "I meant *emotionally* hurt. Apparently, she's all torn up over something and Ruth was going on and on this afternoon about how that's my fault because she wouldn't have encouraged Ella to give you a chance if I hadn't said anything and I don't even know what I said. She convinced my mom it was my fault so she was also telling me to fix it by making you talk to her and somehow they got Jessica on their side because as soon as we got home she was like when are you going to talk to Sebastian? So here I am telling you to talk to Ella because I can't have every woman in my life mad at me over something you did."

"I didn't do anything," Sebastian said, though the idea that Ella was upset did make him feel guilty.

"Then they must be mad about something you didn't do."

Sebastian jogged over and grabbed the ball. If people wanted to be angry that half the town perceived him as a monster, that wasn't something he could fix. All he could do was continue to not get angry himself. That was difficult to do. He passed the ball to Isaac when he wanted to hurl it at him for not letting the subject go.

Isaac did not start dribbling. "Jessica will ask as soon as I get home if you agreed to talk to Ella."

"Seriously?"

Isaac shrugged helplessly.

"I can't, okay? She's afraid of me."

"I…" Isaac seemed confused. He bounced the ball once, then held onto it. "I don't think that's the problem."

"What do you know?"

"Nothing. Except that Ruth wouldn't be so insistent that you need to talk to Ella if Ella didn't *want* you to talk to her."

Sebastian had to admit that made some sense. He knew Ella wasn't really afraid, just had some lingering doubts that she couldn't shake. She couldn't help that and probably felt guilty about it. Maybe if he let her apologize for not being able to get past the reputation then she would feel better. And he knew that no matter what, it had been rude to leave her so abruptly.

"Just tell me you'll talk to her even if you don't intend to so I've done my part," Isaac said.

Maybe if he gave her a few minutes, she'd no longer be upset and everyone would leave him alone. "Fine," Sebastian said. "It won't fix anything, but I'll talk to her so *your* life can go back to normal."

"One more game first?" Isaac held up the ball.

Sebastian nodded. He made only one shot in the second game though.

"I expect more competition next time," Isaac said.

"I'll see what I can do." Sebastian waved and headed to his car. He went home for a shower and more examination. His mom questioned him only with her eyes. She looked at him when he came in as though he might have news. She eyed him hopefully when he cleaned up and left again as though going to see Ella was the only possible reason he might have wanted a shower.

Sebastian circled the block a few times before he parked in front of Ella's house. His feet seemed very loud on the porch, announcing his presence even before he rang the bell.

Naturally, it was her father who answered the door. Mr.

Sweet was not a large man. In fact, he was a head shorter and very thin. But he was intimidating nonetheless because he held all the cards. Sebastian half expected to have the door slammed in his face. "Mr. Jones," he said, "what can I do for you?"

"Hello, sir. I hoped to speak to Ella for a few minutes, if she's willing."

Mr. Sweet wore a serious expression, which he held in place while he looked Sebastian up and down, possibly for a reason his daughter would not be available. Then he nodded and stepped back with a motion that invited Sebastian to enter.

He stepped over the threshold. The house was decorated like something from a catalog page and smelled like vanilla candles.

Mr. Sweet closed the door behind them and stood silently for a moment. He appeared to be intentionally extending the intimidation, but he'd lost a little when he let Sebastian in. Then he actually appeared to be fighting a smile when he said, "It's about time you showed up. You can wait for Ella in there." He pointed to a small room off the entry.

"Thank you," Sebastian said. He went into the room while Ella's dad went the other way, hopefully to get Ella.

The room had a loveseat, a desk and several bookshelves. Sebastian didn't feel he had permission to sit behind the desk, even if it would give Ella a barrier. He made himself as comfortable as the circumstances allowed on the loveseat. He wouldn't be surprised if Mr. Sweet took his time about finding Ella as some sort of punishment. He was only alone for a few seconds before someone entered the room, but it wasn't Ella. It was Mrs. Sweet.

16

There was a knock on Ella's door, followed by her dad's voice. "You have a visitor."

She'd heard the doorbell but hadn't thought much of it. She was expecting a phone call. Sebastian hadn't actually come to her house, had he? She opened the door to face her dad. "Who is it?" she asked.

"Sebastian Jones."

She sucked in a breath that was accompanied by an embarrassing squeak.

"I left him in the den with your mom," her dad said. "Take as much time as you like going down. It'll serve him right." He went downstairs to let her process the news on her own.

Ella expected a phone call. Ruth had assured her that she'd worked on Isaac, and Jessica agreed to keep after him. He was going to get Sebastian to call. Ella had been planning what to say. She'd even written some things out. She couldn't read off her notes if he was there in person. The longer she waited, the more time her nerves had to get jumbled and the more time her mom had to ask embarrassing questions.

She went into the bathroom to check herself in the mirror. She hadn't cried today so her eyes weren't red. That was something. She'd braided her hair over her shoulder before church, and it was still neat. It would have been hard to mess up her hair just sitting around worrying over her phone. Her cheeks were pink from nerves. There was nothing she could do about that.

Ella rubbed her sweaty hands on the sides of her black skirt as she walked slowly down the stairs. The texture of the eyelets might have been soothing if anything could have soothed her.

Ella's dad smiled encouragingly when he saw her, then turned on some music. "We won't hear anything but the music," he said.

The assurance of privacy made Ella nod appreciatively.

"Are you sure you wouldn't rather sit and read a book for a while before you let him off the hook?"

She shook her head, knowing her dad was only trying to help her relax. She smiled a little so it may have worked.

"Okay," he said. "But there are some long ones in the den if you change your mind."

Sebastian was sitting in the den next to her mom. His hands were folded between his knees and one of those knees bounced up and down. Ella took one more step before they noticed her. Sebastian immediately stood up.

"Hi," she said. Her voice sounded natural. That surprised her, but she was fine with it.

"Hi," he said. "I'm only here because I've been informed that you wanted to see me. I'll go if someone made a mistake."

"No. Um, I mean, don't go." She glanced at her mom, who had stood more slowly.

"Sebastian agrees with me that Dawn would make a fine middle name."

Ella tried to keep her jaw from hitting her chest at the pronouncement. Had her mom really been asking him about naming a baby after her?

"In theory," she tacked on, as though that made it okay. "I guess I'll see if I can get your dad to turn down that music." Her mom patted Ella on the shoulder as she left the room.

Sebastian moved away from the loveseat as Ella moved closer to it so that they nearly changed places. That was bad because now he was closer to the doorway. If she said something wrong, he could leave so easily. At least the music volume stayed the same, background for them but prominent in the room it originated.

She swallowed and remembered how she planned to not begin with I'm sorry. That was before he'd been subjected to her mother. "I hope my mom wasn't too..."

He shook his head. "I could tell she was giving me a hard time on purpose. I deserve it if you've been upset."

"I... want to explain," she said.

"You don't have to," he said. "I don't blame you for –"

"Stop!"

He did and looked startled.

Ella had surprised herself with the outburst. She tried to collect her thoughts. "Let me talk, please," she said. "It's hard enough without having to start over after an interruption."

Sebastian nodded and motioned for her to continue.

"I am not afraid of you." That was the first point. Now how did she get him to believe it? "I mean, I'm kind of scared of you because..." She stopped. Telling him she was scared was not the way to convince him she wasn't scared. "Remember how I said I wanted to get you alone to talk about what really happened with Kathy?"

"Alone, with bodyguards," he said.

That was a fair point. "Yeah, but as soon as I was about to ask, I realized I didn't need them. I was afraid that you would get upset and not want to see me anymore, not that you'd get upset and hurt me. I only wanted to hear the details to prove that I... I care about the truth. I am not afraid of you." She'd already said that.

Sebastian didn't really look convinced of anything except that she wasn't the most eloquent speaker.

"Let me explain Friday," she said. "I don't know exactly what you thought, but I thought..." Oh, this would be awfully embarrassing if she was wrong. Her face was flaming already. She took a deep breath and spilled the words out as fast as she could. "I thought you were going to... make some sort of move... like maybe even kiss me and I was so nervous and I get jumpy when I'm nervous and you should already know that. It should have been really obvious that I was just nervous and not flinching to get away from you especially when you've been so patient waiting for me to warm up to you like I need to do with everyone." She'd been looking at the front of his shirt while she spoke and carefully raised her eyes to his.

She'd definitely gotten his attention. His eyes were wide and more hopeful than a minute ago. A smile even twitched at one corner of his mouth.

Ella didn't care if he'd found her speech amusing. She was proud of herself for having gotten it out. And the hint of amusement reinforced her incentive to get to the part where she yelled at him. "Now," she said, "I've been doing nothing but thinking about all this the last two days, and I think you expected me to be afraid."

His eyes narrowed in confusion. Still, he said nothing. He was still being careful not to interrupt.

"Was it... I heard you got a visit from the police," Ella said softly.

He nodded. "I figured it was only a matter of time before you heard that I was hurting my mom."

"And you just assumed I'd believe it?"

"Someone believed it enough to call the police."

"Ruth feels so bad about that," Ella said.

"Ruth?"

"No, no." Ella rushed to correct herself as she realized how that had sounded. "She didn't... She's the one who left the handprint bruise people were talking about, when she grabbed your mom's arm to steady her. She talked to your mom about it so she knew and... Anyway, I knew what people were saying, but I thought if I brought it up at all, you'd think I was fishing for proof I didn't need. So I'm sorry that I didn't say anything. But you... you expected me to be afraid. And now you?"

"Do not know what I'm supposed to say."

Ella laughed but quickly got back to resolving the situation. "You're sorry that you didn't trust me to believe you. And you're very sorry that you didn't give me a chance to explain right away that you only startled me."

He nodded slowly. "Yes. Even without your cues I'd be sorry about those things. I've missed... I've missed the hope that this could be something."

"I... still hope it can," she said. The desire to leap into his arms was strong. It wasn't a romantic thing, just the relief of two friends reconciling. But Sebastian stayed back, still reluctant to make a move towards her. It was up to Ella to close the gap.

She rushed forward before she had time to get nervous and slipped her arms around his back and buried her face in his chest. The newness of touching him was exhilarating, yet familiar. That fresh scent, she'd smelled it before from a distance. It was so much better up close and tangible. She didn't know if she heard his heart or if it was her own pulse pounding in her ears. The moment was one that didn't need words and that was her favorite kind.

"Ella?" he whispered into her hair. "I really am sorry." She felt his arms finally wrap around her. She sighed into the embrace, then stepped back.

"You feel better now?" Sebastian asked.

She nodded.

"Is there anything else you want to say to me?"

She shook her head.

"Do you want to come with me to set up bingo?" His voice was strangely tentative, as though he was asking her out and not just confirming that they still shared an obligation.

"Okay."

He waved a hand to say he'd follow her from the room, and she realized he meant right now because it was that time already. The long hours of waiting to patch things up had suddenly picked up speed. He hung back by the door while she let her parents know she was leaving.

Ella's dad asked if everything was okay. When she assured them it was, her mom jumped off the sofa. She gave Ella a quick hug, then a tiny shove towards the door. The woman's impatience for grandkids was showing again.

Ella stepped onto the porch and nearly tripped over her own feet. It hit her when she saw Sebastian's car that it would be the first time she wasn't meeting him somewhere. Getting into his car put her in his power. It showed a level of trust and a step forward that had been a long time coming. Pretty soon they were going to have to talk about him getting to know her parents. They would expect that. But after everything else, her parents really weren't scary at all.

****

Ella didn't say a word on the way to the church. It was about a two-minute drive so Sebastian didn't say anything either. He was trying to comprehend the fact that Ella was with him. He wasn't trying to bump into her or chasing after her. She was right there and had said she had no intention of running away. It seemed way too good to be true.

They didn't say much when setting up the gym, but it was a comfortable silence. Ella carried tables with him though she'd already proven she could do it by herself. The chairs banged against each other as they pulled them from the rack and unfolded them quickly.

Sebastian needed to pick up his mom, and he was torn between bringing Ella and protecting her. His mom wouldn't resist asking Ella if she'd forgiven Sebastian, if he'd apologized thoroughly, or in some way poking the freshly healed wound. But he didn't want to leave Ella when the mended fence felt stronger than before. It seemed to be a good time to follow her lead. What did she want to do?

"I guess I need to go get my mom now," he said.

"I'll wait for you."

She'd wait. Those were beautiful words. He could keep his mom from bugging her and still spend some time with Ella. "Okay," he said. "Where will you wait?"

She nodded towards the playground. "I'll sit on the swings or something. Come find me when she's settled."

The sooner he left the sooner he could return. Sebastian watched Ella walk away for only a moment before he hurried home for his mom. She was in the kitchen putting her dishes in the dishwasher.

"You ate?" he said.

"Yes, thank you." She looked him over for a minute. "I assume you set up the gym already."

"Yes."

"Did Ella help?"

"It's ready," he said. "Are you?"

She smiled at the impatience and pointed to the walker with her purse and sweater already hanging from it. He helped her to the car and then to her usual seat for bingo. Two other players had arrived so he wouldn't be leaving her alone. He held the sweater for her to get her arms in it, then placed the walker within reach at the end of the table.

"I'll be back for you at nine," he said.

She nodded. "Tell Ella I said hello."

Sebastian walked outside not caring that his mom could read him like an open book. Ella was waiting for him. The thought made him so happy it had to be obvious. But there was another thought demanding attention. He'd been trying not to think about it while they had important things to talk about and important chores to accomplish. Now he was free to remember that when Ella had been lecturing him for not trusting her and explaining how he'd been a fool to think she feared him, she'd said she thought he was going to kiss her.

She said that made her nervous. She did not say it was too soon or too awful. She didn't say she was nervous about pushing him away. She only said nervous.

There she was, sitting on a swing as she'd said. She had to tuck her legs well underneath herself to keep from dragging them. She planted them firmly to stop the swing when she saw him coming. She waited for him, looking small and vulnerable on the low swing. But her smile spoke only relief that she was no longer alone.

"That was quick," she said.

"I was motivated."

She cast her eyes to the ground in front of her. It appeared she was about to stand so he held out his hand to help her. She didn't flinch. She took his hand and pulled herself up without looking higher than his chest. She was still nervous.

Truth be told, so was he. Her grip on his hand loosened so he let go and brought his hand slowly to her face. Her skin was soft, and she trembled. He saw the reaction for what it was because she made no move to escape or pull away. He kissed her as gently as he could and vowed to be careful with her every step that lay ahead. Not because she might be afraid and not because she was as fragile as some people might think. The woman had strength when she needed it. He would treat her like glass only because he knew that she was far more valuable.

17

Ella felt a strange internal war as she walked down the hallway holding Sebastian's hand. She didn't want anyone to see her holding his hand, but she thought if she only held on tighter it would be okay.

Sebastian pulled them to a stop just before they entered the room for the Friday night meeting. He raised her hand to his lips and kissed the back of it before he let go. His eyes were less hesitant than in the past, confident that she was uncomfortable with the PDA because it would draw attention to her and not because it would draw attention to her being with him.

Ella ducked into the room and went straight to her usual seat next to Ruth.

Sebastian followed, but he headed towards Isaac, who was still standing. "Grace with your mom tonight?" he asked.

Isaac nodded.

Jessica said, "She better not wake her up."

"She was kidding," Isaac said.

"Mom threatened to wake up the baby?" Ruth said, laughing.

Isaac looked around the room to include everyone who was now looking at him. Eric and Julia were there. Next to them was a guy Ella didn't recognize but who seemed to know Eric. Two younger women were in the circle as well. Ella knew their names were Tiffany and Tori. She couldn't remember which was which though. They were sisters who were both short and blond. They'd been coming for months but only sporadically.

"She was kidding," Isaac repeated. "Now that Grace is starting to have a more regular bedtime, we don't want to keep her up for these meetings. My mom was giving us a hard time about *finally* letting her babysit now that she sleeps the whole time. She joked about waking Grace up to play as soon as we left."

"Aw. She's so cute." That was either Tiffany or Tori.

"Have you met his mom?" Eric asked. "She's more fierce than cute."

"Uh…"

Tiffany or Tori looked uncertain until the other one elbowed her and said, "He knows you meant the baby."

Several people chuckled.

Eric shook his head. "I shouldn't try to be funny."

Heather entered the room already waving to everyone.

Ella put her hand up to wave back, but the gesture became much smaller when she realized the person with Heather was Luke Wasserman. She dipped her chin and hoped the blue frames made her embarrassing speech less prominent in his memory. She hadn't been wearing glasses the last time she saw him. But she tensed up mostly for Sebastian's sake. The one other time Luke attended a meeting, he got angry at the sight of Sebastian and walked out. He did not appear particularly happy to see Sebastian this time. He set his bearded jaw as he walked past, making a wide circle to an available chair. But he did sit down.

Heather signaled a not-as-subtle-as-she-thought thumbs up to Ruth and Ella before she sat next to him. She'd told them recently that she and Luke were "friends" now. It was unclear whether there was more she wasn't saying or simply a hope of more. It was nice to see her happy either way. A year ago, Ella hadn't really liked

Heather. She seemed snobby and gossipy. But without the influence of some former friends, she was becoming more pleasant to be around.

"Congratulations!" Heather said, wagging a finger between Ruth and Gabriel.

"Yeah, I didn't get to tell Gabriel congrats yet." Julia offered a nod of approval.

"Are you making an official announcement tonight?" Heather asked.

"Yes, we're engaged," Ruth said simply. Her glow didn't seem dimmed, even though she'd been looking forward to an announcement that obviously wasn't necessary.

The only sign of surprise around the room was inside Ella for not predicting that everyone would already know. She caught Sebastian's eye. His lit up with a smile that said he'd been waiting for her to look his way. She felt warm and mushy as he came to sit beside her. She surreptitiously scanned the room to see if anyone noticed. It occurred to her that there wasn't much to notice because Sebastian almost always sat beside her. Maybe she deserved a bit of the sarcasm he'd thrown at her last week.

"Are we saving a date yet, Baby Ruth?" Isaac asked.

"No, Ike." Ruth paused to let the tit for tat nickname sink in before she really answered his question. "We're thinking December or January but won't have anything concrete until we find out when the church is available and such."

Gabriel flipped open his notebook in what they all recognized as the signal that it was time to begin. "I'm feeling like maybe we dive in with an Our Father today," he said.

Everyone smiled, put their hands together, and followed his lead.

Ruth opened a laptop. "It's movie night," she said. "Well,

sort of. We're going to talk about St. Ignatius of Loyola, and there's a movie about him that's pretty good. But it's long. I think we'd have to spend at least three weeks on it to watch the whole thing and still have time to talk some. And some of it, you guys will thank me for skipping."

Ella nodded to herself. She and Ruth had already talked about the movie at work.

Gabriel rolled his eyes though. "It's not that graphic."

"Some things are better left to the imagination," Ruth said.

Jessica winced. "Oh, I know St. Ignatius was injured in battle, and I think the doctor had to rebreak his leg, maybe more than once, to set it properly. Did they show that?"

Ruth said, "Yes."

Gabriel said, "No," at the same time.

They looked at each other.

"They didn't really show it," Gabriel said. "Only enough to know what was going on."

"Yeah, it wasn't bloody, but there was a man screaming in agony, which I think is worse. But the parts where he feels the need to punish himself with a whip are the hardest to watch."

Several versions of "ouch" were muttered around the room.

"We're not watching that part," Gabriel said.

"Uh… so what *are* we watching?" Eric's question was a clear hint that it was time to start something.

"Right, right." Ruth tapped on her laptop before she turned the screen around. "So quick recap while you position yourselves so you can see. St. Ignatius was born into a wealthy family and became a soldier with dreams of glory and fame to go with his money. But as Jessica said, he was injured. Reading scriptures was one of the few things he was able to do while stuck in bed and that facilitated his conversion. This part of the movie is right after that where his family doesn't exactly approve of his new ideas and plans, and they try to talk him out of it. We're going to watch a few scenes and then talk about some times when other people, maybe our own families, haven't been supportive or even disrespected our faith." She checked to see that everyone was situated and then pushed play.

For some reason, Ella had been expecting a low-budget snoozefest, but it was a quality production. She was quickly sucked into the portrayal right up until Ruth stopped it again, which happened to coincide with Joseph and Emily's arrival.

"Is the movie over?" Joseph asked. "That's the only reason I could talk Adam into coming." He gestured over his shoulder as his brother came in behind him.

"That was just the first part," Ruth assured him. "Plenty of entertainment left."

Isaac jumped up. "We need another chair."

"That's okay," Joseph said as he claimed one of two empty chairs. "Emily can sit on my lap."

"Agh." Heather made a gagging sound. "You two are not allowed to be that cute in here."

Emily snorted. "It'd only be cute for five minutes. Then Joseph's leg would fall asleep, and he'd drop me on the floor."

"I only drop people on purpose." Joseph gave Eric a taunting look.

Eric laughed and said, "All the time." He was also training in hapkido but was significantly outranked by Joseph and Isaac.

There was some shifting during this exchange to make room for another chair in the circle. Once everyone was seated, Gabriel gave Ruth a nudge.

"Our first topic, which you can address whether or not you saw the movie clip, is... um... Would anyone like to share a time when you've gotten some pushback for your faith?"

Eric looked at Julia. "That sounds like a question for you."

She tipped her head thoughtfully. "Yes, I did experience a lot of friction with my parents when I first converted. But I know now that was partially my own fault. I kind of treated them like they were idiots for not seeing what I saw."

"I think I…" One of the sisters bit her lip as she stopped speaking, looking at Julia to see if she was interrupting.

Julia nodded at her. "Go ahead, Tori."

Ella made a mental note that the one with shorter hair was Tori.

"I was just going to say that's sort of understandable," she said. "Sometimes I hear a passage that's so powerful that… I like the parable of the wedding feast… sometimes I hear something and wonder how anyone can hear the same thing and not be moved. Sometimes it seems so obvious."

"We all hear things through the filter of our unique experiences though," Sebastian said. He opened his mouth again but closed it without adding anything.

Ella could guess why. Luke had shot him a glare that suggested he did not have permission to speak.

Joseph thought he'd said enough. "Exactly." He pointed at Sebastian, then addressed Tori. "I was actually on the other side recently. I came out of church feeling disappointed in what I thought was a very boring homily. Don't tell anyone I said that," he said quickly with a smirk. "But it was about keeping priorities in order and felt, to me, like nothing we haven't heard a million times. I went to my parents' house for lunch later. As soon as I walked in the door, my mom was like, 'Boy, that was a great message today.'

"I like the early Mass and they like the later one so I honestly thought we'd gotten different homilies. But we talked about it, and she was struggling with something and needed the reminder. It hit her differently because of her different circumstances."

"That's similar to the way the same Bible passage can make you feel different at different times in your life," Isaac said.

"Huh?" Heather gave him a confused squint.

"Well… for example… let's say a person reads something that makes him feel better about the fact that he's still figuring things out. A few years later, he reads the same words, but this time he remembers and realizes that he hasn't grown much. Now he's uncomfortable because he let the comfort turn into complacency."

"I get that," Heather said, looking ever so slightly awed.

"Brilliant as usual." There was an interesting mix of admiration and exasperation in Ruth's voice. "But you're so off topic. Again."

"It's all related to faith," Joseph said. He grinned at his sister. There were no heart flutters, but Ella could still appreciate that he was a nice-looking man. He'd teased Ruth a few weeks earlier that they were never off topic. They were only letting the Holy Spirit lead them places she hadn't intended. It was kind of hard to argue with that.

Ruth stared at him for a moment. "Have you ever gotten pushback from someone in your family?" she asked.

Several people laughed at the way she twisted the question from its original form before they got back on track. No one shared anything particularly poignant. Emily and Heather remembered friends mocking them for wanting to go to church *every* week. Tori said that her uncle had married a woman who occasionally tried to save family members from the "wrong" Christianity.

When Ruth started another clip from the movie, Adam was teased about his ability to keep up with the moving pictures. He took it well. Ella suspected he actually appreciated the pretense that he'd been avoiding the young adult group because it was too academic for him and not because he'd been nursing a grudge against his siblings.

The next set of questions was somewhat light. But then they watched a darker portion of the film and got more serious. Ella didn't say a word the whole meeting. It was probably the largest group they'd ever had. While speaking up in that setting would have been intimidating, she mostly found that there was enough conversation that she was content to listen.

The only disappointment was that Sebastian was also fairly silent. And that was tempered by curiosity. She knew he was talking less than normal to avoid upsetting Luke. The curiosity was about whether or not she had anything to do with his attendance. Had Heather talked Luke into coming on her own? Or had Ella's spontaneous outburst actually hit a nerve? Had she convinced him to grudgingly give Sebastian a teeny tiny chance? The idea that she might have left any kind of impression pricked her pride but also made her try harder than usual to avoid eye contact with Luke as the group broke up for the night.

Most people left quickly amidst a flurry of wishes for a good week. Isaac rolled a table away from the wall before Jessica tugged his arm. She seemed anxious to relieve their babysitter. Gabriel and Sebastian assured him they would take care of the tables, and they did have them back in place in barely a minute. Ella helped Ruth arrange the chairs around them. Then the four of them headed down the hallway together.

"Do you have any interest in watching the rest of that movie?" Sebastian asked Ella.

"Kind of," she said.

"It really is pretty good," Ruth said, "but she's as squeamish as I am so you'd have to allow some turning away or fast forwarding."

Ella nodded and tried not to picture burying her face in Sebastian's shoulder during the disturbing scenes. She didn't want to be caught wearing a goofy smile while thinking about disturbing scenes.

"I think my mom would like it," Sebastian said. "I was thinking if you come over early on Sunday, all three of us could watch a movie before dinner."

"Okay." She and Ruth usually left Emily's place between three and four. The timing worked well, though Ella could hardly believe the shy girl who'd never had many friends was planning her Sunday around three different visits.

Gabriel got to the door first and held it for the others before he locked it behind them. There was some waving as he followed Ruth to her car and Ella moved farther down the lot with Sebastian. She'd gotten a ride with him that week.

Ella stopped on the sidewalk in front of his car. If they were going to have a few minutes to talk, she'd rather do it by the church than in front of her house where her mom might not be able to keep herself from frequent glances out the window.

"You look lost in thought," Sebastian observed.

Ella felt her face turning red. She'd begun to picture the good night kiss she didn't want her mom to see. "I, um… What makes you think your mom would like the movie? Is she not bothered by… unpleasant stuff?"

"She can handle *pretend*," he said, with just a hint of condescension. "And I've gotten the impression that this unpleasant stuff is like five minutes of a two-hour movie. Mostly I just know she's a fan of St. Ignatius."

"Saints have fans?" Ella wrinkled her forehead. That seemed an odd way to put it, though she couldn't immediately think of a better word for admiring the life of a saint.

Sebastian shrugged. He seemed to be thinking the same thing. "She credits him for bringing her back to the church. My mom was raised Catholic but pretty much abandoned any kind of faith around the time she finished school. During her recovery, someone pointed out the parallels between the twelve steps and the spiritual exercises of St. Ignatius. That's what brought out her real faith. I've read some of his work, too, and… You know, I guess we're both fans of his." He smiled at the admission. "It's a good plan anyway because if we're watching a movie, she won't be able to ask you a bunch of personal questions."

"I like your mom," Ella said. "The questions don't bother me."

"Yet," he said. His manner was apologetic.

Ella thought it was unnecessary, but she had to admit she didn't know his mom that well *yet*. She hadn't been alone with her. That would likely be scarier. With Sebastian in the room, his mom was amusing. They both were. It was obvious they loved each other very much, but they seemed to be constantly on the brink of a huge sigh. Ella kept these thoughts to herself. She'd already said she liked his mom, and it seemed safest to end the subject there.

"Ella, I want to ask you… something."

The hesitation made her brace for something difficult.

"Remember when I saw you at Granny's Shelf?" he said. "Were you actually interested in that glass bunny or did you only go in there as an excuse because you saw me coming?"

Ella bit her lip and looked down in embarrassment. But she'd required harder honestly from him. She bravely met his eyes and said, "Can I say both?"

"If both is the truth." He seemed more confused than doubtful.

She took a breath. "I saw the bunny first. I was really thinking about going inside for a better look when I saw you. That caused me to run inside a lot faster than I would have otherwise."

Sebastian smiled at her admission. He appeared strangely relieved to hear she'd been trying to hide from him. "Good," he said. "I was afraid you didn't really want the bunny." He moved closer to his car as he spoke and opened the back door.

Ella was baffled until he reached for something near the floor and came out with a familiar glass object displayed in the palm of his hand.

"Oh!" she exclaimed. "*You* bought it?" She remembered when she went back for the bunny, and the scene made a little more sense. Mrs. Johnson had thought Sebastian bought it for her. And then her brain registered the fact that he had. It triggered a sappy smile.

"Do you want it?" He made no move to give it to her.

Ella stepped forward and took the bunny from his hand. "Thank you," she said, then reached around to give him a quick hug.

He responded with a kiss that was not quite as quick.

Ella smiled as she got into the passenger seat, holding the glass figure on her lap. She realized that it was now going to make her think of Sebastian almost as much as her grandmother. She hoped that would be a story that only got better the more they added to it.

www.ingramcontent.com/pod-product-compliance
Lightning Source LLC
Chambersburg PA
CBHW031345170626
46807CB00002B/832